Blood on Lake Michigan

By

Michelle Gartner

Text Copyright © 2014 by Michelle D. Gartner

Published by Michelle D. Gartner

ISBN-10: 0990621219 (paperback edition)

ISBN-13: 978-0-9906212-1-8 (paperback edition)

Cover Photo and Cover Design Copyright © 2013, 2014 Jerry M. Gartner

CHAPTER 1

Loving someone makes us blind to who they are. When we love deeply we don't see people as we should. My best friend Kelly understands me like no one else does. She knows everything about me, even my deepest, darkest secrets. But loving her makes me blind to how dangerous she is to me.

Kelly is a vampire and that makes her the top dog. Kelly is an apex predator in our world. She is above man eating tigers and great white sharks on the human food chain. I would rather swim across a shark infested pool, than face a single vampire alone. A shark might shred you to pieces, then swallow you and be done with it. But a vampire will toy with you, psychologically damage you, and then slowly bleed you dry over days- maybe even weeks, simultaneously torturing your mind and breaking your body before you finally die. I would take on a pool of sharks any day over tangling with a vampire, especially a vampire I didn't know.

Despite the risk of being best friends with a vampire, my bond with Kelly is strong, because we each have a supernatural secret that makes us kindred souls. Granted, my secret is not the same as being an immortal, blood thirsty creature of the night, but because we both have our secrets, we have become more than friends. We have made a pact to be each other's safe harbor in a world opposed to freaks and monsters.

I met Kelly in ninth grade study hall. She was quiet and different from everyone else in our school- like an exchange student from a different world. Most of the new freshmen were loud and noisy in a 'look at me' sort of way. Then there was Kelly, who materialized into places like smoke. When she walked into study hall that first day, no one saw her take a seat in the back of the room except me. I was drawn to her- a moth trapped in a web.

On the surface Kelly was dark and brooding, even for a teenager on a diet of angst and bad music. She appeared indifferent behind a veil of dark hair, but my gut instinct said she was checking me out with all the curiosity of a cat playing with a mouse. I tried to act casual looking back at her, but she caught me flipping back and forth several times, and turned the tables on me. The next time I did it; she stared right at me, until I quickly buried my head in my algebra book. After a few minutes of pretending to read, I peeked back at her hoping to catch her looking the other way. But she was waiting and winked at me, chasing me right back into my math book.

When I did get up enough courage to look back once more, her eyes were piercing and drove straight through me. Frightened, I almost fell backwards out of my chair; because it was at that very moment I knew she was literally inside my head. I couldn't explain it, but this girl

2

was reading my mind by using some sort of supernatural power and it freaked me out.

When I discovered what was going on, I tried harder to ignore her. But the creepy sensation of someone else inside my head, slowly picking at my brain and rummaging through my thoughts was unnerving. And after a few unbearable minutes, I jumped up and ran out of study hall- headed straight for the nearest bathroom.

Slamming into the door of the last stall, I vomited into the toilet. Afterwards - I was relieved, because my thoughts were my own again. I was shaking, sweating and breathing hard- but otherwise I could tell I was alone. I sat down on the cold floor to catch my breath, but instead screamed long and hard! The noise echoed off every wall in the bathroom, crashing back into me.

"Shhhhh," she said. "You're okay- I won't do that again."

"What are you talking about?" I sputtered, "Get away from me!"

Scared, I tried to get up and rush past the strange girl, but she grabbed me and pushed me back into a seated position. My mouth dropped open- she was unnaturally strong like she was on steroids. And she was smiling, as if I would be glad to see her, when really I just wanted to get away from her. Her smile wasn't normal- it was big and toothy; the grin of a rabid dog before it's about to sink its teeth into a human hamstring.

Without easing her grip on me she said, "Hi- I'm Kelly. You're Sinead right."

I nodded. The nausea I had earlier was creeping back up on me as she talked. Her voice was buttery, smooth- manipulative almost. And she kept talking-oblivious to my stomach burbling and the soft pounding in my head. "It's nice to finally meet you."

"I promise I won't do that again."

"What are you talking about?" I asked.

"I won't read your mind, unless you want me in there…" she tapped her head and smiled, this time less like a dog getting ready to bite and more like *a friend.*

I couldn't imagine wanting or voluntarily allowing someone to read my mind. Not only was it was a total violation, but it felt horrible. It was like eating ice and getting the longest, slowest brain freeze imaginable while someone pokes at your frozen brain lobes with an ice pick. Done gently it was an ice cold fingertip trying to massage and coax private thoughts out of mental thin air. Either way, having someone read your mind was a mental root canal.

"I didn't mean to do that to you." The girl loosened her grip on me and sat down next to me, gently putting one of her arms around my shoulder, in case I passed out.

"Okay," I nodded. I had little control over the situation and wanted to get back some personal space from her if I could. "I need some air. Will you let me up so I can go outside?"

"Sure," she said, "can we talk?"

Kelly helped me to my feet, leading the way. Every time she smiled I winced. It felt like I was waiting to be poked for a blood draw.

Outside the fresh air made everything less claustrophobic, less like I was in the grip of a dangerous fiend and more like I was on a walk with a friend. Once we found a secluded park bench, away from school, the two of us spent the rest of the morning talking until late afternoon.

Born in the late Victorian era, and changed into a vampire in 1906 when she was seventeen, Kelly had lived in three separate centuries. She didn't have to convince me she was a vampire, I knew she was different. She knew so many fascinating firsthand details about the past; about historical events and places that I could only read about in books. Her life so far, was one non-stop adventure, and mine paled in comparison. When Kelly said she still felt like a kid even after a hundred years of living, I was envious. Who wouldn't want to live forever in a body that never aged and had supernatural powers? And to travel the world, and do anything she wanted, it was amazing.

Her story was spellbinding, but I could tell she was being intentionally vague about certain subjects; glossing over the details of the three vampires that she lived with including another older, female vampire that posed as her guardian. I got the distinct impression that this subject was off limits and I wasn't in any position to pry for more information.

After telling me about herself, she let me ask her a bunch of questions, such as the obvious- like the effects of sunshine, garlic, and crosses on her. The one thing I didn't ask about- was blood drinking.

When I was done playing twenty questions, supernatural edition, Kelly explained that she wanted to get to know me, when she tried to read my mind back in study hall. And it caught her off guard when I put up a fight against having my mind read. The more I resisted her; the more she poked back. She didn't mean to be forceful; and apologized again, but I was uneasy knowing that my brain could be picked like a lock by a vampire.

The sun traveled across the sky casting long shadows on us as Kelly talked about living in the twenty-first century. For centuries vampires were content to be monsters on the edge of human society, but this was changing. The modern world was difficult- with all of its tracking of people and up to the minute news updates online. Technology made it harder for vampires to hunt people as there were less humans on the planet untouched and accounted for by technology. Some vampires had lost the will to exist, finally ending their own lives because they didn't want to live in the information age.

I was genuinely charmed by Kelly. She wasn't an ogre- she was someone I could be friends with if I could get past the trust issues of being friends with a vampire.

At the end of our first conversation, Kelly told me that that her desire for blood was uncontrollable and that she drank blood every day. Of course that freaked me out being a blood-filled mammal myself. It wasn't the best note for her to leave me on, but I guess she figured I could handle the truth. I didn't take it well.

In the early days before our friendship took off- I thought Kelly was toying with me. I figured she was getting around to drinking my blood at her leisure, in some sort of sick game. And my response was to avoid her and pretend she didn't exist. On the other hand, Kelly acted like were old friends. She was clueless that I didn't want anything to do with her, because she had stopped reading my mind, like she promised.

I couldn't help it; every time I thought about being friends with a vampire my blood ran cold. If her thirst for blood was so out of control- why didn't Kelly get on with it and have at my six pints of blood? Better yet, why hadn't she drained all the students and faculty in one enormous, gruesome bloodbath? Back then- I had a lot of nightmares.

The sky was a brilliant shade of blue when I entered the building. Birds were singing- even indoors. In the halls, students shoved each other and laughed. Throwing my backpack under a desk, I took a seat in the front of home room. The teacher was already at the board, his back to us writing. Turning to make morning announcements- Mr. James tried to speak, but his words failed him. He struggled for air and choked. His eyes rolling back into his head before he slumped to the floor dead! I wanted to scream, but first I looked to the rest of the students for their reactions… they were all dead too, sprawled over their desks in grotesque poses.

My blood turned to ice in my veins. She was in the back of the room. I could tell because she was probing my mind. Finally, I looked back at her, but only because she compelled me to. Kelly was waiting for me to see her for what she was- a blood thirsty monster!

She was a vision of horror and unsatisfied hunger. Blood splattered her face and dripped down her chin making horrifying inkblot patterns on her desk. One of these small patterns peeled itself off the desk; a grim, bloody butterfly that flitted towards me. Hypnotized, I watched it flutter about the room before landing above my head. That's when I peered down to see Kelly poised above me about to sink her teeth into my neck!

Fortunately- the nightmares always ended before Kelly drank my blood…

Someone said being drained by a vampire was a painful ecstasy that will make you crazy and break your will to live all at once, besides killing you. Kelly didn't tell me that- I was pretty sure I read it on the internet. But regardless of where I got the information from, I didn't want to find out if it was true. I hated to imagine Kelly drinking other people's blood, let alone mine!

I was making myself crazy, but it was a normal reaction to a vampire trying to pursue a meaningful relationship with me. We weren't really friends. We never did anything together and I rarely saw her outside of school. Kelly never came to my house to hang out, because I never invited her over. And that's because I believed there was this rule that you had to invite her kind into your house before they could come inside. And that was never going to happen if I had anything to say about it.

It's not that I didn't think about Kelly outside of school. In fact, I was morbidly obsessed with her once I left school. I felt safer there, believing that Kelly wouldn't try to drink my blood with all those people around watching. But at night and at home alone, it was different. While doing homework I had anxiety attacks. Sometimes I shivered and shook for no reason. And I couldn't shake this creepy sensation that I wasn't alone or the feeling I was being watched. I kept the curtains tightly closed, afraid of what might be out there waiting in the dark. I imagined people and things, sitting outside on the ledge waiting for me to open the window to invite them in for a drink of my blood.

Several weeks of this absurd cat and mouse game went on, until one day in early October when Kelly asked me about

Halloween. 'What was I going to dress up as? Was I going trick-or-treating?' Before I could even answer, Kelly decided it would be fun for the two of us to go trick-or-treating together.

That was the straw that broke the camel's back. "Get it over with! Stop playing with me!"

"What are you talking about?" she asked flashing those weird manipulative eyes at me.

"Just eat me, or drink me. Whatever you plan on doing- get it over with!"

Kelly clenched her teeth and peered down at me from the bridge of her nose. She couldn't believe it. But I was too angry about her wanting to make liquid lunch out of me, to be frightened.

"I am not going to bite you. Don't you trust me? I thought we were friends. I told you everything. Do you think I tell everyone I'm a vampire?"

She glared at me, hurt.

"Well- you read my mind wrong. We could never be friends!"

With those words- I was the monster. I wanted to apologize, but I didn't. Instead I held my ground and watched her disappear.

From then on, Kelly ignored me. It was as if I didn't exist and I was relieved at first. And I reassured myself that I did the right thing, because she was a real life vampire after my precious blood.

But after a few days of getting the cold shoulder from Kelly, something changed. There was a hollow feeling in my chest. I pushed away my only friend. And this wasn't that extreme or far from the truth. Because I didn't have any other friends and I was a loner since grade school. Being born an only child with no friends, I blossomed into a full grown wallflower in high school. But that changed when Kelly wanted to be my friend. The problem was- that the only other person in the world who wanted to be my friend, besides my mother was a vampire.

CHAPTER 2

The school hallways were crowded with vampires, witches and zombies. I almost fell over at least four caped Draculas looking to sink their teeth into the necks of cheerleaders. Kelly wasn't wearing a costume, but she looked happy for the first time in weeks. I was still suspicious of her, but secretly pleased that she seemed happy.

I didn't dress up in a costume for school either. There wasn't much reason to go to the trouble since there weren't any classroom parties in high school. I was pretty shy anyway and I didn't want anyone at school to see what I was going to wear later when I went trick-or-treating with the kids I babysat for.

That night at home- I put on the Marilyn Monroe costume I ordered off the internet. At the time it seemed impulsive and exciting. But it turned out that impulsive didn't translate into exciting like I had hoped. Out of the package, the costume was two pieces- a blonde curly clown wig that wasn't sexy and a white halter dress made from thin polyester fabric. It didn't help either- that the seams looked like they were sewn together by a trained monkey handling a sewing machine. Maybe in a dark club it would be sexy. But under glaring porch lights, while trick-or-treating- people would mistake me for Ronald McDonald's loose, little sister.

Downstairs the phone rang while I applied makeup- dark red lipstick, heavy mascara and a large penciled on fake mole. My mom picked up the phone, so I ignored it and went back to creating drama with an eyebrow pencil. When I was done with my makeup, I tried on several pairs of heels before deciding on a pair of white Chuck Taylors. Sneakers would be more comfortable than heels and I could run after the kids I babysat if I needed to. As I laced up my shoes, I debated if padding my bra would help my cause or hurt it.

My mom called up the stairs, "Sinead."

"What?"

"Mrs. Thompson called; Becky is sick, so you don't have to take the kids trick-or-treating."

"Augh!" I cried as I flopped back on my bed.

So much for free candy! And I wasted good money on a stupid costume that I was embarrassed to be seen in and was too thin to wear outside in the cold anyway.

"What was that?"

"Nothing," I replied.

But it was huge. I was stuck at home without a backup plan. I didn't want to miss out on Halloween. I was in high school, my trick-or-treating days were numbered. Taking Becky and Daniel out was a good excuse to score some free candy.

Sulking, as the sun went down; I decided it wouldn't kill me to go out. Even if I wasn't bold enough to go up to doors alone, it beat pouting at home. Jumping up, I pulled a heavy coat over my costume, and adjusted the blonde wig a final time before heading out.

Outside, the air coming off Lake Michigan was biting. I pulled my coat close and walked quickly to keep my blood moving. Without the kids tagging along, I could walk faster and could go wherever I wanted. The only problem was- I didn't know where to go. Not wanting to be entirely alone on Halloween, I walked down North Street towards the lake and followed the crowds of trick-or-treaters filling the streets.

Swarms of children lined the sidewalks, and costumed kids shouted 'trick-or-treat' at open doorways. Candy rained down into open sacks and little faces were beaming as they admired their bulging bags and pillowcases. I tried not to be envious of the little kids getting their bags filled with treats, but it was hard.

Calvary Cemetery emerged ahead- halfway between my house and the lake. For a split second I hesitated before crossing the street to get to the sidewalk that ran parallel to the cemetery. I could still walk away-everyone else in the area stayed away from the cemetery, but that was because there were houses on the opposite side of the street to stop at for treats.

I almost missed the early warning alarm, until I felt the sense of dread creeping up in the background that went with it. The warning was a low familiar buzzing, a noise like flies swarming and eating. The noise would make me nauseous if I continued, so I had to force myself through the crosswalk and onto the sidewalk. Despite the alarm, I walked on, concentrating so I wouldn't fall, and moved forward.

On the other side of the street, the ground buckled beneath me. Undeterred, I hurtled forward, reeling down the road, putting one foot down after another. I walked the full length of the block without falling and turned left at the corner, skirting the other side of the cemetery. The effort made me break out in a cold sweat, but I kept going.

There were voices above the buzzing. First- a few distinct voices and then there were too many to count. The voices were soft at first- a few whispers in the dark but as more voices were added, there was a crescendo of shouting. Hundreds of forgotten voices were competing for attention.

My stomach lurched into a rhythmic pattern- a rusty see-saw going up and down. Leaning over- I gripped the iron cemetery fence as sweat poured out from under my wig. I pulled the wig back to get some air on my scalp and steadied myself before trying to move again. But I was paralyzed and clung to the fence like a madwoman.

"Are you alright?"

I gripped the fence tighter and swayed in loose circles. Two strong hands steadied me before prying me off the rusty fence from behind. I staggered when I was set loose from my death grip. And then the hands pushed me down the sidewalk towards the cemetery gates.

"Sinead, are you sick?"

My eyes rolled up as waves of nausea hit me over and over. I was helpless, like a boat passenger struck with motion sickness. Ahead there was a break in the iron fence and the big metal archway of the cemetery revealed itself. I was being ushered inside the cemetery and I resisted the hands on me.

"Hey, I won't hurt you!"

"Not in there," I cried. "I never go in there," I whispered before darkness came.

"I promise I won't hurt you..." Kelly said as she tightened her grip on me, carrying me down the car path towards the crypts.

I was only unconscious for a moment. In the pitch black darkness of night a bright light emanated from within me and I was covered with a blanket of warmth that wasn't there before. It was like being shot full of energy. I was upright again and floated a few feet above the tombstones.

The buzzing had stopped momentarily ringing in my ears only to be replaced by the most horrible noise known to human ears. Part glass shattering, part microphone feedback and nails on a chalkboard- the horrific cry came from deep inside my lungs. As I howled and screeched, my body swayed and I took off in flight towards the lake as if powered by a combination of rocket fuel and the terrible noise pollution coming from inside me.

Within seconds the shrieking stopped and I was out cold- lying on the shore of Lake Michigan, four blocks from the cemetery. When I came to, Kelly was leaning over me muttering and cursing.

"Whoa! Are you okay, Sinead?"

I nodded and waited for my eyes to adjust to the dark again. Staring down at me was a skateboarding zombie who was assessing my vitals.

"You're a zombie, with a skateboard?" I asked.

"Yeah, it's a good way to get around fast on Halloween. I'm quite good on a skateboard."

"Wouldn't it be easier to fly around like a bat?"

"Easier, maybe- but I like being down here with everyone."

Kelly moved my head off the ground to keep the sand out of my hair. I appreciated the gesture, even if it meant she was awfully close to my throat. It was oddly peaceful laying there with my head in her lap looking at the stars.

"Wow! How about you? You're keeping secrets. What just happened?" Kelly was squinting at me as if she was examining me for microscopic clues.

She would never guess in a millions years... I exhaled loudly and said, "You're going to laugh..."

Kelly glared at me, "I'm over a hundred years old, so I am sure I will find this really hard to believe."

"Banshee," I whispered, "I just went banshee."

"You're a BANSHEE!"

"Shh- you don't have to announce it to the world," I shrieked back in a voice that was like my death howl only a hundred decibels lower.

"I don't get it. What's a banshee? Are you a ghost or a witch- sort of a cross between the two? Well- that explains some things... witches hate vampires. I wondered why you had an aversion to me. Most people are falling all over themselves to get near me. It's an occupational hazard of being a vampire," Kelly winked.

"I'm definitely not a ghost... you can tell I'm not dead can't you?"

"Definitely," she licked her lips.

I tried to ignore that slip but it was unsettling. "I'm not a witch. I don't have any magical powers."

"No? You don't call what you just did- having 'magical powers'?"

"No, not really I don't have any control over that. It's like sneezing. I don't practice witchcraft or have magical powers I can control. I'm definitely not a witch. I don't know how it works but it has something to do with fairies. I have a little bit of fairy blood in me," I said.

"Really... Is there such a thing as fairies?"

"I don't know. I guess so- everything I know about being a banshee comes from things that happen to me or whatever I find on the internet."

My head throbbed, but the worst was over. And Kelly had seen me transform into a banshee. Becoming a banshee had happened so infrequently in the past that sometimes even I forgot how different I was from most people. Suddenly, it occurred to me that Kelly and I were sort of on even ground. Maybe we had a lot more in common than a predator-prey relationship.

I was shaky when I tried to sit up. Even though my secret was out, I didn't want to be caught dead in her arms. Kelly pushed me upright, to help me and I scooted around in the sand to face her.

"I know the fairy thing is weird. I don't know that I believe in fairies or if they even exist. But there's got to be some explanation for why I am a banshee and the general belief is- that a banshee is a woman with fairy blood in her veins. Surprisingly, there isn't a lot of information out there on banshees. You can find out a lot more about vampires."

"Oh well that's not surprising… that's because vampires are a threat. Banshees don't hunt humans for food, do they?"

"No- I suppose not. I don't want to drink blood. I'm not much of a meat eater, but if I do start craving blood just shoot me."

"It's not that bad."

"What's not bad?"

"Drinking blood- you get used to it."

My stomach was an acidy volcano. I burped when she said that…I could taste something nasty in the back of my throat and grimaced. It was time to change the subject.

"I think I'm adopted," I said.

"What do you mean 'you think', don't you know?" Kelly asked.

"Well, my parents aren't different; they're… really normal. But I don't know how we can be related, when I am like this. They've never said I'm adopted, so it must have been a closed adoption. I've seen my birth certificate, it has my parents' names on it, but things don't add up. I think they're hiding something. Here's something- my name is Sinead and we aren't even Irish."

"Hmm," said Kelly. "Did you ever ask them about your name?"

"Well, no," I admitted.

"Okay," said Kelly, "maybe you should ask them. It might clear up a lot of things; maybe you're named after a distant relative. Your name isn't that strange."

"Maybe you're right."

"So what if you're not a banshee. You can't believe everything you read online. What if…Maybe you're …"

She was accessing the archive of known fantasy creatures… werewolves, witches, ghosts- she was going through the rolls but coming up empty.

"What? Come on Kelly- do I look like a werewolf? You can't walk through me- I'm not a phantom. I looked it up online and it was right there on Wikipedia... I'm a banshee."

"Okay- so you looked it up online- what did you search for, 'why do I scream in cemeteries'?"

Sarcasm didn't suit Kelly, and made me defensive. "Yeah- something like that. I don't remember exactly, but it's the only thing that fits. Let me tell you about the first time I turned into a banshee."

"When I was a little girl, I seemed *pretty* normal. One reason I didn't find out I was a banshee until later was because my parents never took me to any funerals. I guess they wanted to shield from death... oh and another thing, I've never had a pet."

"Obviously your parents aren't Victorian, I went to a lot of funerals when I was a child," said Kelly. "I understand what you're saying about funerals though, but what's having a pet got to do with this?"

"Most pets don't last forever. If I had a pet die on me, I would have been locked away in a nut house for kids.

"Anyway- about seven years ago, I was playing in the front yard when all of a sudden I heard a swarming sound. It was quiet at first, but then the noise got louder and louder as if it was coming straight at me.

"I thought a swarm of flies was after me- or maybe it was mosquitos. I tried to get away from the sound, but when I looked around, there was nothing in the air. All I saw was the neighbor's dog running to me from across the street.

"Mrs. Murray was our neighbor then and she had a little cocker spaniel that she loved to pieces named Cheesy. Cheesy wanted me to give him a treat or play with him, when he saw me outside. But when Cheesy ran across the street to get to me, he got hit by a car.

"Everything was in slow motion," I said as I paused to catch my breath. "Right before Cheesy got killed- I tried to stop him. I yelled 'STOP CHEESY STOP!' But that's not what came out. What came out was a horrible screech and I almost passed out."

"You mean like tonight- a banshee shriek. What did Mrs. Murray say when you screeched?" Kelly asked. Her eyes were wide.

"Not much- she was really upset about her dog. She didn't see me until later. She was in the street with Cheesy dying in her arms. My mom ran out of the house because she saw me lying on the front lawn like I was dead. No one heard the shrieking, except me. I couldn't forget it. I was scared. And all I could think was, 'what's wrong with me?' I was a little kid and I felt broken inside. It was kind of traumatic- and there was no one to talk to about it."

"I can imagine," Kelly said. She laid an icy hand on top of mine.

In an instant, Kelly was different. She was no longer soulless or had calculating undead eyes like a shark. Instead- she understood and she knew how scared I was.

"That's strange that your mom and Mrs. Murray didn't hear you yelling. There is no way anyone within a few blocks of us couldn't hear you tonight. Good thing it's Halloween. How could anyone miss that?"

"Well yeah- I have thought about it a hundred times or more. I don't think anyone heard me then, because it was one small dog dying. And maybe because I was younger, I didn't make as big of a bang as I do now. I have a tendency to go off louder when people are involved.

"The first time it happened I didn't want to believe it. For a while I told myself that what I heard was the car tires screeching. But when it finally happened again years later- I couldn't pretend like it didn't happen…something was wrong with me."

"Does this happen often?"

"No- it's weird… sometimes I expect to change because of something around me and nothing. And then other times, it hits me when I least expect it. I hear the buzzing noise and feel nauseous. Then BAM! I let out a horrible scream and pass out. I always have enough warning to get somewhere safe when it happens, though.

"The strange thing is people die every day and I don't change. I don't howl or shriek over the obituaries. But I can't predict whose death will make me keen. It's called keening- what I do."

"That is odd- that you don't change every time. I wonder what makes you change if it's not simply because somebody died," Kelly said.

"Just so you know, I hear the buzzing noise every time I am about to change. It's a loud noise that sounds like thousands of flies swarming and feasting on dead things."

"Eww, that sounds unpleasant." Kelly was grossed out by flies feasting on dead things… she was a vampire that drank blood and dressed for Halloween as a zombie that feasted on human brains… that was strange.

"We need to find out more about banshees," said Kelly. "You need someone to help you figure this out."

"Yeah- well if you want to be my friend you might want to be more careful where you take me. I wouldn't have changed tonight if you didn't drag me inside the cemetery. There are at least nine thousand bodies in Calvary and I have a crazy way of responding to death even after the fact. I don't go into cemeteries. If I hadn't bolted, I'm not sure how long I would have stayed in there shrieking and rattling the gates. I get really weird and compulsive inside cemeteries.

"I'm trying to build up some resistance to being around already dead people but until then I avoid going inside graveyards."

"I'm sorry Sinead, I didn't know. I saw you hanging onto that fence and thought you needed help."

"I know," I said, "but at first, I thought you were dragging me in there to bite me."

I wanted to bite my tongue when I said that. I just remembered- I was avoiding Kelly at school because I was afraid of her making a meal out of me.

"You still worried about that?" Kelly asked.

"Why wouldn't I be, you told me you had an insatiable desire to drink people's blood, remember?"

"Hmm- as I recall, I said blood, not human blood. I forgot to mention that I don't drink human blood?"

"No. You left that little detail out. What are you trying to tell me- that you are some sort of vegetarian vampire or an ethical vampire?"

"Ethical, not exactly, but I don't get around to drinking human blood."

"And why is that?"

"It … well it tastes funny, okay."

"What do you mean it tastes funny? You're a vampire, you like blood don't you."

"Yes, I like blood, Sinead," Kelly sighed. "It's just that with all the junk food and preservatives and awful things people eat- not to mention drugs, alcohol, and other chemicals inside people's bodies- human blood doesn't taste right anymore."

"What do you mean by 'anymore'?"

"I haven't been drinking human blood since the early fifties."

"Really?"

"For the most part; I hunt animals because their blood tastes much better than human blood. I may have slipped up once or twice since then, but generally speaking people are off the menu. There have been a few, odd health nuts that I find wildly irresistible, but I don't want to drink their blood simply because their vegan and run marathons, that would be immoral. I like people, not merely to drink- Sinead. In case you haven't noticed I'm a person too."

I kept my opinions on blood drinking to myself. Kelly was kind to me and I didn't want to be mean to her anymore. Maybe she only drank animal blood, but I was queasy about Kelly drinking *any* type of blood. I wondered what kind of animals she drank from. We lived in Wisconsin, so I pictured Kelly attached to a cow in a dark pasture. No- that probably was not how Kelly fed herself. I suppose she hunted deer, everyone in Wisconsin hunted deer. This was fruitless and gross; I dropped the subject from my mind.

"I'm tired and cold. I want to go home and get in bed. Whenever I change into a banshee, I feel drained. Could you help me up?" I asked through chattering teeth.

"I can do better than that- I can have you home in a minute."

Before I could protest, I was cradled by a block of ice. Kelly picked me up and pushed my head down so I couldn't see. It was a bit scary in her arms, not knowing what was going to happen next, but oddly enough I was comfortable in her arms. She smelled peculiar and earthy, nice even.

Kelly traveled at high speed. I didn't know if she was running or in flight. She was going so fast, I was afraid to look even if she let me. Anyway- I was so tired, that only two things mattered to me. One- I wanted to get into my nice warm bed and two- I hoped the blood on her shirt was just makeup.

As soon as she took off, Kelly stopped again. I pried my face from her ripped jacket, confused. We were already in my back yard, behind the garage. Kelly put me down.

"Do you want to come in?" I couldn't believe I invited Kelly inside my house.

"Not tonight," Kelly said, "I have to be somewhere."

I was crushed. Was she was giving me the brush off?

Then Kelly said, "We are friends now, right."

"Yes, definitely," I replied.

Kelly hugged me briefly before she left; it was so fast, her movement, like a hummingbird that I almost missed it.

"I won't hurt you Sinead, I promise."

I went inside that night believing her. But the truth is- it was an extraordinary leap of faith on my part.

CHAPTER 3

Once high school was over, Kelly decided we were going to travel the world so I could find myself. She felt that the only way for me to really find out about being a banshee was to get out there and kick around the dirt looking for answers. We would be archaeologists, only not digging up dinosaurs and past civilizations, but looking for answers in the supernatural world.

In the meantime, I still had two years of high school to finish. Waiting around for the future to arrive wasn't so bad though, because Kelly made every event and holiday extraordinary, and even the mundane days were thrilling. Being best friends with a vampire was exciting without even leaving the state.

It was six weeks into our junior year and everyone at school was making plans for Halloween. I was excited too, because Kelly had made plans for us. She wouldn't tell me what they were, but I managed to piece together what she had in mind from bits and pieces of conversations we had in the weeks leading up to Halloween night.

First- Kelly was going to have our costumes custom made. Obviously Kelly had a lot more money than I did so I didn't argue with her. And I didn't object to her choice of costumes either, when she suggested that we dress in matching superhero costumes. Her reason for the superhero costumes- was that wearing masks would keep us anonymous on Halloween night. But I kind of thought the matching costumes were Kelly's way of announcing our friendship to everyone. And that was fine with me, because I loved being her friend and I didn't mind being her sidekick.

Unfortunately- Kelly wasn't interested in the 'getting treats' part of Halloween night. I didn't understand why she wanted to play tricks on people, but I suppose the idea of ringing doorbells and begging for candy wouldn't appeal to a vampire. Whatever she had planned though, I was game, because I had a lot of fun being with her.

Kelly had strange motives, until you considered she was a vampire, and then things made more sense. And it wasn't just that she was a vampire that made her weird. Besides that, Kelly was backwards, because she was born when Queen Victoria was still alive. Sometimes she would say something absolutely bizarre that she picked up during the Jazz Era or while living through the Depression.

That's why I liked her so much- despite her hundred years of experience and old fashioned ideas; there was a perpetual teenager trapped inside her undead body who was fun and spontaneous. It was her sense of adventure that I loved the most, because I craved adventure too. I was sure Kelly could find something more exciting to do than hanging out with me, a girl in high school, and I was lucky to be her friend.

As it got closer to Halloween, Kelly leaked out a little more of her secret itinerary for Halloween. Kelly wanted to toilet paper some of her neighbor's houses, which seemed a little anticlimactic and off the wall- at least to me. And besides toilet papering her neighbors houses, there were some kids from school she wanted to terrorize- I assumed by jumping out of trees and confronting them in dark alleys when they least expected it. I wasn't sure exactly, because she didn't actually say what she would be doing. But I did know there was someone in particular that she wanted to scare.

None of her 'tricks' would be mean or dangerous. Everyone she wanted to scare was at least a teenager. And teens loved getting scared, based on the movies we saw. I wouldn't have gone along with her if she wanted to sneak up on old people or little kids. Not only was it mean, but I couldn't risk someone croaking on us with my uncontrollable condition.

I would be doing very little other than watching her pranks and giving out moral support. And what could possibly go wrong when we were both masked? That was the beauty of the superhero costumes; no one would ever find out our secret identities. And since Kelly had everything carefully planned out, it would be fine. I didn't have any better ideas anyway, and in the past, my

Halloween plans bombed. In the meantime- all I had to do was convince Kelly that I needed candy like she needed blood.

I didn't find out until a few days before Halloween that Kelly's climactic finale to the end of the night was me going off on a group of unsuspecting teenagers in all my banshee glory like a paranormal fireworks display.

"How are you going to pull that one off?" I was upset when I found out what her real plans were.

"Someone has to die for me to freak out. Did you plan on killing anyone I know just to get me to shriek? This has the makings of a horror movie," I said. "Have you seen the movie *Carrie*?"

"No, is it about Halloween?"

"No, not really, listen Kelly- I am not sure I want to do this," I said.

"Don't worry Sinead, you'll be wearing a mask- no one will know it's you. You told me that when an animal dies you hardly go off at all. It will be spooky, harmless fun. I'll be there to keep you safe. This will be fun," she repeated.

"For you maybe, but not for me and your victims," I said. "Wait you're going to kill an animal? Oh gross- that's sick!"

"Don't be so dramatic, we've been friends for a couple years now, you know I drink blood from animals every night. Since when has this become an issue? I just plan on having a drink while you are around and we'll see what happens. I have everything under control." She winked at me.

This sounded like a commercial for Las Vegas. Kelly watched too much reality TV and it gave her bad ideas. She said watching TV was how she found out how the other half lived. I tried to explain to her that normal people weren't on television, but she didn't care.

Kelly probably got the idea about toilet papering houses from watching TV too. Toilet papering houses was weird. I didn't want to go to jail for vandalism on top of being exposed as a banshee freak. Next - she would have us graffiting the town with 'Vampires Rule!'

"Do you have someone in mind you want me to scare? What did this person do to you? And how do you know when or where this person will be on Halloween?"

"That's complicated, but the simple answer is, you take one part mind reading and two parts vampire persuasion and I can pretty much guarantee my victim will be where I want them, when I want them within a small window of a time. It's not an exact science, but I can be ever so persuasive." She made an L shape with the fingers of both hands and put them together in front of her face like a small window. Then she smiled through her little finger window at me.

When she smiled, I was putty in her hands. It should have been obvious to me that she was using vampire persuasion on me so I would go through with her plans.

"What if I don't want to do my thing, it's not fun to go banshee.... Even a little shriek is painful."

I was pouring it on, maybe it wasn't exactly painful. But the buzzing and the nausea were like having a sudden attack of the flu. And the worst part was that it ended in a climax of screeching that sounded like me vomiting knives on glass. That probably explained why I passed out afterwards. I definitely didn't want to pass out in front of anyone I knew on Halloween night.

"Don't be a killjoy; this will be fun. What other time of the year can we act crazy and not get in trouble? We're practically given an open license to scare people on Halloween. Besides all I'm asking for is one little spooky banshee howl. For me, you will do it for me, right?"

"I'm supposed to say no to peer pressure, especially manipulating vampire peer pressure."

Kelly quivered her lower lip at me and smiled. I saw fangs back there, something she usually keeps hidden. I rolled my eyes at her.

"We're not children anymore," I frowned, "my parents will kill me if I wind up passed out in jail."

"Don't be such an extremist, nothing is going to happen to you, you're with me."

"So you say." I wasn't at all convinced that my best friend hadn't gone off the deep end.

This wasn't like Kelly, after she found out I was a banshee, she kept me from death, accidents, cemeteries- and anything else that might accidentally cause me to change. She knew I felt like a horrible monster when I was a banshee. And I thought she understood how important it was to me not to transform in front of people. I was completely vulnerable as a banshee and I worried about what could happen to me when I was unconscious after an episode. I don't know what changed Kelly's mind about me transforming into a banshee in front of people, but I still wanted to keep it to myself, especially around the kids we went to school with.

When the big night arrived, Kelly was waiting at my back door with a huge box. "Open it up," she said when we were upstairs in my bedroom.

I was surprised Kelly was excited about a couple of superhero costumes. Slowly, I opened the box and peeked inside- it wasn't primary colored spandex. Instead layers and layers of pale gray tulle and lace poured out of the box. Dropping the lid on the floor, I pulled out a dreamy, endlessly layered gown and held it up. It was gorgeous!

From the bodice up, the dress was a conventional formal gown. But portions of the skirt and sleeves were carefully shredded to make it look ancient. It was ethereal and lovely- the perfect dress for a night of ballroom dancing by a zombie princess.

"What do you think? I designed it myself."

"It's not what I was expecting. It's amazing. Is it for me or you?"

"It's yours, do you like it?"

"Yes- I love it, thank you. But I thought you wanted to dress like superheroes?"

"I changed my mind. You're not my sidekick."

"Yes, yes I am- it doesn't bother me. Where's your costume? What are you going to be?"

"A vampire."

"Just a vampire?"

"What do you mean 'just a vampire'?"

Her eyes twinkled; she wasn't upset.

"You know what I mean. You can't go as a vampire that would be like me wearing a sweater tonight. You're not dressing as Count Dracula or…?" I couldn't think of any famous female vampires- except for that nasty countess who bathed in human blood. And she was actually human and not a vampire.

"No- you'll see when I come back… I'll meet you in twenty minutes behind your garage."

The gown was even more amazing when I put it on. It was unlike anything I had ever worn and way more expensive than I could afford. The top of the dress had a form fitting bodice of gray velvet that fit perfectly and was accented with lacy sleeves that billowed at the wrists. The bottom of the gown had tulle underneath that filled the full skirt out and made it float. The dress was beautifully made and then skillfully tattered so that it looked authentically old. It had a haunting beauty that couldn't easily be copied.

Included with the dress was a pair of ballet slippers, a masquerade ball mask with ribbon ties, and matching tights. I shuddered remembering the Halloween I had dressed as Marilyn Monroe in bare legs under a thin halter dress. Kelly hadn't missed any details, making sure I would be warm and masked. At the last minute I put on a little makeup and pulled my hair up.

All of my trepidation and reasoning went out the door when I put on that dress. Once it was on I walked through the door of a fairy tale... I wanted to be a part of Kelly's crazy, messed up plans even if it meant transforming in front of my classmates. And who cared about getting candy, when we could do something so wickedly cool that it would have people talking about it to their grandchildren fifty years later.

Kelly was already waiting for me behind the garage. When she stepped out of the shadows, my jaw dropped, she was wearing a top hat and tuxedo with tails. She was stunning- a vaudeville performer or a carnival barker only there was something slightly menacing about her. Her costume suggested a night of frightening entertainment.

"So this is a vampire costume," I said. "You look like Marlene Dietrich."

"Yes- but you know she would have had to copy my style, I'm a tad bit older than her," she said winking at me.

Showing off, Kelly flipped upward- planting her feet on the underside of the garage overhang and hung upside down held by nothing but the soles of her feet. She laughed when I swatted at her while she danced back and forth like Fred Astaire dancing on a ceiling. I had no idea how she did it, but I knew she had a powerful mind and could will most anything to happen… that was what made her so dangerous and fun.

"Come on show off, get down- and let's have some real fun," I said.

"Show off- I'm not showing off, you will be the main attraction tonight! Just wait," Kelly said as she jumped down and took off towards the street.

I had to run to keep up with her. Not knowing the way, I followed close behind until Kelly stopped at a small, plain house. Once there- she positioned me on the sidewalk directly in front of it before she walked ten feet up the path. Turning dramatically, Kelly clapped her hands and immediately there was a loud KA-BOOM followed by a flash and smoke…Dense gray smoke completely enveloped the little brick house. Faint shadows moved in the thick smoke.

After a brief moment, a dark figure emerged from the fog and Kelly lifted her hands dramatically and said "Ta Da!" as she made a sweeping circular motion with her outstretched hands. The cloud of smoke disappeared in one large swirling vortex simultaneous to her arm motions and there in the clearing air behind Kelly was a house completely covered in toilet paper!

I laughed and applauded as Kelly took off her top hat and made a deep bow. Her papering work on the house was amazing. What would have taken a mob of pissed off high school kids at least an hour; she had managed in less than thirty seconds. The house was mummified.

Kelly repeated her 'magic trick' at several houses, adding little flourishes and making each one different. At one house half the lawn became a minefield of pink flamingos, another, a riot of funny garden gnomes. In the meantime- Kelly was amassing a large audience of trick-or-treaters. Kids crowded around her, admiring her handiwork and following her from house to house. I was getting nervous. It wouldn't take long for one of the neighbors to whip out a cell phone and call the cops on us.

At her last house, Kelly finished to a huge round of applause from a large crowd that had gathered to watch. When she was done hamming it up and bowing I grabbed her by the elbow and told her we should make a quick getaway.

"Don't worry I can outrun the cops, even if I have to carry you," she whispered.

That was what I was afraid of. I didn't want to outrun the cops; I was hoping they wouldn't be on to us to begin with. Her black tuxedo made her ninja like in the dark shadows, but I was a huge moving tulle target in my gown.

Finally, Kelly broke free from her adoring fans and followed me into the nearest alley. Once we were far away from the scene of the crime I asked her about it.

"So how'd you do it?"

"That's a magician's secret- I can't give away my secrets."

"Oh give me a break, I know you did it with your super speed and some sort of smoke, flash bomb- but where did all the toilet paper come from?"

"I had the toilet paper and flamingos already hidden in the bushes," she shrugged. "Next year, I need a camera," she said obviously pleased.

"What did those people do to piss you off?" I asked nodding back in the general direction of the mummified houses.

"I'm not pissed at anyone; I'm just having fun..." said Kelly.

"There's something going on there, but that's okay if you won't tell me. We all have our little secrets. What's next on your diabolical agenda?"

"Let's go scare some kids."

For the next hour, a vampire girl jumped out of trees- and off garage roofs and second floor balconies into the midst of unsuspecting trick-or-treaters. It was comical and at the same time I sort of felt sorry for the kids. I was pretty sure more than one kid peed their pants that night. Fortunately, Kelly only targeted kids middle school age and older, and if there happened to be a little kid caught in her ambush, she reached into her vest and handed them a couple of big pieces of candy to soothe them.

As the night progressed, I worried again; knowing it would be my turn next to frighten the masses.

"Are you okay?" Kelly asked.

"Yeah- I'm fine; I'm cold all of a sudden… Are you going to tell me what's going to happen next?"

"Do you still want to go through with this?"

"Well, first you have to tell me what it is you want me to do."

"There's someone from school I want you to scare. I'll tell you why later. They'll be coming this way shortly."

"Okay- but why couldn't you scare them yourself?" I asked.

"Because I think you're scarier than I am."

"Really?" I found this hard to believe.

"Yes, I think you can do a better job than I can. Are you still up to it, because we need to move quickly?"

Kelly's face was lit up with anticipation. She had done a lot for me and I hated to let her down, especially at the last minute.

"Okay, I'll do it."

"Great," said Kelly, "here's the plan…"

The girl Kelly wanted to scare had already left her house and was on her way to pick up her friends. And once they were all together, the group of friends would be walking to a party held at the lakefront. Prior to the night, Kelly had suggested to several of the boys in the group that they walk through Wildwood Cemetery on the way to the party.

"Wait a minute Kelly- this is going to happen in a cemetery."

"Yes, this is going to be so cool."

"Why are we doing this in Wildwood? Can't we do this somewhere else?"

"We're going to do it in there, because you got upset about me killing an animal around you... remember. This is going to be so scary!" Kelly bobbed up and down, excited.

I didn't remember it exactly the way she had described it. I was grossed out about her drinking animal blood. And I wasn't thrilled about her killing an animal to get me to change. But what I had said was 'that's gross', not 'that's gross so let's do this in a cemetery instead...'

This was going to be so scary for me. I didn't realize this was going to happen in a graveyard. I tried not to think about what she was proposing- but I had already formulated a picture in my head. Kelly wanted me to rise from the tombstones and scare the living daylights out of a group of teenagers that we knew from school. But what she didn't know was that I was terrified of Wildwood. A

45

few years ago when I changed into a banshee in front of Kelly that was at Calvary Cemetery- a small four block open cemetery in the middle of a quiet neighborhood near my house.

Wildwood was a different type of cemetery altogether; it was a least twice as big as Calvary and very isolated even though it was in the middle of town. Surrounded by trees on all sides, the cemetery was a dark and lonely place. And the truth was I had never actually been inside it because I always made sure no one drove me through there on a short cut through town. There were probably hundreds if not thousands of more bodies buried in Wildwood then there were in Calvary Cemetery. And to top it all off, there was another large cemetery adjoining Wildwood, called Lutheran Cemetery. It was a double cemetery!

I was hyperventilating when I found out Kelly planned to do her Halloween night scaring in the mother of all cemeteries. Steadying myself, I gulped and tried to stay focused on what I agreed to do.

"Okay Kelly, I don't need any directions on what to do once we get in the cemetery. But what will happen to me when I pass out? Don't leave me in Wildwood all night please."

"I won't- I already made arrangements to keep you out of the way. You'll be back home in bed before you know it. This is going to be great."

Terrified, I followed Kelly to the cemetery. It was completely silent as we walked up the hill in Kiwanis Park, except the pounding of my heart, which Kelly could obviously hear. Above the hill was a stand of trees that hid the entrances of the two large cemeteries. My knees locked up and it was difficult to move.

"Nervous?" Kelly asked.

I nodded a little bit, and made a grim smile at her to show her I was still in. Continuing, we walked by the train bridge and past the last street corner before the cemetery. When we turned the corner there was a densely wooded hill and a sign marking the entrance. Kelly stopped to give me some last minute updates on the group's progress.

"They're in Lutheran cemetery now, past the mausoleums and walking towards the middle."

"Okay," I said.

There it was- that familiar faint buzzing noise; it wouldn't be a problem for me to make the transformation from teenager to pissed off banshee.

"There's an old Victorian tombstone on the edge of Wildwood. It marks the grave of a sea captain. It's a large tombstone with a statue of a woman on the top. She's holding an anchor and searching the horizon for sailors. On it is written, 'Homeward Bound.' You can't miss it. One of the boys is leading them to the tombstone right now."

"Why would he do that?" I murmured.

"Because I planted the suggestion that the tombstone is haunted and even gave him a story to tell the others. He's telling them about the haunted tombstone as we speak."

"Okay Kelly- don't say anymore. Lead me to the tombstone when you are ready for me and I will do my thing. Just don't leave me in the cemetery alone okay?"

"I won't leave you alone- I promise. They will be at the grave in less than five minutes. Are you sure you will transform?"

"Definitely, I already hear the buzzing noise. It will definitely happen if you lead me in there."

We climbed the car path that led into Wildwood, the buzzing in my brain getting louder and louder with each step. I started to reel up the path like a drunk as waves of nausea hit my stomach. Kelly could sense my distress and gently pushed me up the drive steering me towards the lawn of the cemetery.

Once inside we headed towards the older part of the cemetery where the Victorian gravesites were hidden in back. In the distance several small lights were bobbing between the tombs and headed our way. A few of the kids were holding flashlights, but as they got closer to us the lights were extinguished. Kelly was directing their movements with her mind and she suggested to them that they put out their lights.

A tall tombstone with an etched schooner and a lady searching the heavens materialized in front of me. I crouched behind the monument, it was as Kelly had described, and she immediately disappeared from my side when I ducked behind it.

Muffled voices were speaking, buried in the earth, trying to be heard. My feet barely touched the lawn as I held on to the headstone to keep from floating up. Wrapping my arms around the cool stone, my fingertips clawed into the etched dates. Anchored to the tall monument, I waited as the group moved steadily in the dark towards the tomb of John Thompson.

After a few moments of clinging to the marble, I could faintly hear one of the boys retelling a ghost story to his friends. As he got nearer, I concentrated on his voice to keep myself steady and focused on the task ahead.

"The rain lashed the boat, the winds howled and finally a large wave crashed over the bow submerging the whole front end of the boat. More than fifty men were onboard that night and not a single man survived.

"Only one body was ever recovered. That was the body of John Thompson. And when they finally found his body and pulled it out of the lake, they could hear a woman wailing over the wind and waves. It was a strange noise that went on for three straight nights. Every night the woman howled over Lake Michigan, terrifying the people of Sheboygan. Until the day of his funeral and when they finally put John Thompson's waterlogged body into the ground.

"Legend says the howling woman was a siren who saw John Thompson on the boat and picked him out of all the men onboard to be her lover. She was the one who made the huge swell come up from the middle of Lake Michigan to toss all the men overboard. And when all the men fell into lake, she went straight for John, leaving the rest of the men to drown in the turbulent water. The siren was so in love with John, that when she tried to make love to him under the waves, he drowned as well."

Despite the chilling tale, several girls giggled. One of the boys made deep rasping noises- his impression of a man moaning and drowning during sex.

They were close, I could tell by the crunching of their shoes in the grass and leaves that they were near where I was hidden behind John Thompson's tombstone.

"After they buried him in the ground, the siren came out of the lake and when her feet touched dry land she turned into a banshee guarding his grave. And if you try to get close to his tomb she will rise from the earth and shriek to warn you away from her lover's final resting place."

A few seconds of deafening silence ticked by before the boy added ominously…

"The thing is- if you hear the banshee howl you will be the next to die!"

That was my cue. And feeling sufficiently rotten enough to levitate and howl, I closed my eyes and let go of the headstone. I floated up like a helium balloon. This time I would try to control my ghostly performance.

A soft muted light emanated from me.

"Did you see that?"

"What?"

"There's something there behind that grave."

That's when I floated from behind John Thompson's tombstone and softly howled into the wind. As I levitated higher and higher, I concentrated my shrieking towards the terrified voices and got louder. I rose above the granite woman standing atop John Thompson's tomb and shrieked hard.

Two girls shrieked in unison back at me. For one bizarre moment we were a trio of terror screeching in harmony on Halloween night. Two of the boys had seen enough and made a break for the nearest exit. And when the shrieking girls saw the boys escaping, they followed in hot pursuit screaming the whole way down the car path. I wanted to follow right behind them- I wanted out of the cemetery too… but there were still other classmates left to scare.

I pulled my attention from the teens that had escaped and back to the scene in the cemetery… there in front of me stood a girl alone and petrified with fear. She was stiff and motionless. Neither her lips nor legs would do anything to help her out of the desperate situation. She was in shock. And I didn't know what to do to get her moving, short of shoving her, except shriek louder. With any luck, her eardrums wouldn't be shattered.

I howled louder, directing every ounce of lung power I could to getting her to move, but the girl wouldn't budge. And then things spiraled further out of control, when another boy appeared from behind a large shrub. He wasn't empty handed. The boy had picked up a large tree branch and was wielding it with menace. I knew what he planned on doing with it. He was going to hit me right out of the sky, but for the moment he was as dumbstruck as the terrified girl. And he stared up at me with a curious expression and the tree branch hanging limply at his side.

I started to panic. I was trapped in Wildwood Cemetery with a petrified girl and a boy with a large stick, who was about to whack me into the next world when he recovered from the shock of seeing me go banshee.

This was not going well. I was on the verge of passing out- and where was Kelly? This was her horror movie moment and she was nowhere to be found. The more I panicked, the less I clung to reality. Another burst of adrenaline and I was nauseous. My eyes began to swim up to the sky, and my head rolled down. I welcomed the blackout...

Something small and black whizzed by my face before I went entirely under.

I was only out for minutes but it felt like I was unconscious for years and then woke up in another decade. The air around me was stagnant and moldy and added to the effect that I had come to in the past. I tried to fill my overworked lungs with a bit of fresh air but was met with a dense, dusty air that smelled ancient. Feeling claustrophobic, I coughed and wheezed to expel the old oxygen reviving me and tried to suck in clean air. And even though I was awake again and in a quiet place by myself, something was terribly wrong- despite somehow being rescued from the two petrified teens in the cemetery.

Gathering my wits, I tried to figure out my surroundings. Something was above me that was hard, flat and smooth. Like a mime in a closet- I felt to the sides of me and found the exact same surface. Horrified- I was in a box!

I was in a coffin- buried alive.

And I knew exactly who had done it.

I wanted to scream and scream until help came, but there was nothing left of my voice, not after my last ditch effort at shrieking at the teens.

At first the grim reality of my situation made me break out into a cold sweat and gripped me with a new panic. And a gruesome thought crossed my mind- would Kelly make a snack out of me when she got back. My heart beat so hard it rippled in painful waves up my neck. But then something quietly told me that everything would be all right. Relaxing all the tense parts of my aching muscles, I melted into the wood that rubbed into my spine. It was probably macabre to resign myself to my fate as an end of the night Halloween treat for Kelly, but I didn't care anymore. It beat being whacked out of the sky by a high school boy with arms like an orangutan.

From inside the coffin, I wondered about the boy that came to rescue the petrified girl. Who was he? I recognized the girl; she was Melanie Walker, a popular cheerleader at school. The boy was a mystery though, and if Kelly let me live, I definitely wanted to meet him. There was something puzzling about him. I liked the way he looked at me, even though he held a really large stick pointed in my direction.

While I contemplated boys and being buried alive, a strange phenomenon took place. My body was still encased inside the coffin, but something inside me- my soul or maybe my spirit rose up for a couple of brief moments. Whatever it was, wanted to rise and fly up out of me and break free from the box holding me.

It was as if my spirit had a mind of its own and wanted to leave this place to explore other realms. But I didn't want it to leave and willed it to stay. I wasn't sure what would happen if I let this part of me go. If it left would I die? Could I be dying? Maybe there wasn't enough oxygen in the coffin.

But besides being afraid of death if I became untethered to my soul, another practical reason kept me from allowing this part of me to leave. Above me I sensed the remnants of skin and bones- a dead body and one below me still buried in their coffins and rotting in the crypt. I was between two old dusty, dry corpses; and I didn't want my curious spirit to pass between the two.

That was when I hit the panic button again, because my brain couldn't relax. It didn't like that I was in a coffin, shelved in a mausoleum, like a stashed away sandwich for my best friend to snack on later. To calm myself, I tried counting backwards from a hundred.

38, 37, 36... something scraped the outside of the vault- my coffin was being pulled off the shelf.

Please let it be Kelly, I didn't want anyone else to make a meal out of me... 35, 34, 33 – my heart was beating so hard in my chest I wanted to scream. I needed to compose myself and be brave if I had to act quickly for the zombie apocalypse waiting outside. 32, 31, 30... My coffin was lowered onto the ground with a soft thud. 29, 28, 27... Augh! What was out there? The lid creaked open and a dark figure hovered over me in the shadows.

A sliver of moonlight glinted through the stained glass window of the mausoleum onto the pale figure illuminating the blood smeared on her face.

"Oh my God Kelly- you killed them! I didn't know you were going to kill them!"

"Shhh- I didn't kill anyone. After you passed out I grabbed a quick bite to eat. But then I heard you coming to. I didn't want you to freak out because I put you inside a crypt."

"You couldn't have found somewhere better."

"We're in a cemetery; where else could I put the body?"

I wasn't smiling.

"Okay- sorry…maybe this wasn't ideal… but I didn't know how long you would be out. I thought it would be okay to stick you in here, where no one would come across you. I don't know how your fainting spells work. I was afraid to wake you up. Are you okay? You're not mad at me?"

"Yeah- I'm okay." I pulled myself out of the coffin, taking the hand she offered. I wanted to throw my arms around her neck. I wasn't sure if I wanted to hug her or throttle her. My brain was still divided. I decided to let it go for the time being.

"Tonight was incredible- I was able to control myself most of the time, until I passed out. I might actually be getting the hang of this and guess what?"

"What?"

"I had an out of body experience while I was in there," I pointed a thumb back at the coffin that I was glad to be out of.

"Really- I get those all of the time… mainly in Mr. Field's Sociology class." Kelly made snoring noises.

She was still trying to make me laugh, but I was too busy digesting everything on the walk home to be mad. It was actually a small miracle that I was able to walk on my own and that I wasn't pissed at Kelly… In the past, every time I transformed, I would pass out from the exhaustion of what my body went through to become a banshee. But that Halloween was different, I could control being a banshee if I didn't panic. And there was obviously more to what I could do then howl and levitate. There were a lot of possibilities I hadn't explored yet.

We stood in the doorway of my house, inside the sunroom, while outside in the dark night, older kids were still shrieking wildly and having fun.

"Here," said Kelly producing a pillow case half stuffed with candy. "To the victor belong the spoils."

"Where did you get that from?" I asked.

"One of the boys dropped it in the cemetery. I knew how much you wanted candy tonight. Next year we'll go trick-or-treating."

"Gee- thanks. I feel a little weird eating it though…"

"Well- I'm not going to eat it. Enjoy," said Kelly.

That night I went to bed late- happy and grateful for my friendship with Kelly. She was hard to understand, but I appreciated the way she embraced life and wanted to make everything an adventure.

Drifting off to sleep in the middle of a sugar coma, I imagined Kelly and myself exploring hidden places in the world. We would travel to faraway lochs in Ireland to search both magnificent castles and isolated huts looking for the key to my existence. We would discover moors inhabited by phantoms. And spend nights in places I would be afraid to stay in on my own. Maybe it was selfish that I thought only of myself, but I would never make it very far without her help. I didn't have the money or courage to take a trip across the Atlantic on my own. And I needed her because she would be the one keeping both real and imagined demons at bay in the real world.

Kelly was my very own Joan of Arc, a knight in shining armor dispelling the trolls and dragons that stood in my way. She could open the doors of opportunities that I couldn't open on my own.

My imagination turned the corner and became lost. At the next point, an old crone with a familiar face motioned to follow her to a hut on the edge of an isolated loch. She knew me and wanted to tell me about my family. But when the old woman saw Kelly coming up the hill behind me- she was visibly upset and kept Kelly outside.

I tried to tell the woman that Kelly was with me, but she shushed me.

"I know the source of evil your friend is," the crone said. "Don't trust her; promise me you won't put your faith in the oldest evil on earth…"

I nodded to pacify her, and sat down at the hearth. It felt awful to leave Kelly outside, but I wanted to hear what the old woman had to say. Ignoring my discomfort, the old woman threw something under the dying embers that immediately revived old flames. The heat set off a reaction and the liquid bubbled and boiled in a cauldron that was for cooking or witchcraft.

Mesmerized by the steaming bubbles popping and sputtering over the flame, the old woman began to weave and spin tales. Beginning before recorded time, she mixed myth and legend into an intoxicating brew. Then she moved on to recorded history, concentrating on the Middle Ages and the wild places in Ireland where banshees appeared frequently. I clung to every word, trying to memorize the phrases that held meaning.

The woman talked through the night. And when morning came I knew everything. The sun shone on my face as I met a breathtaking sunrise over the loch. I greeted the day happy and whole. Kelly had stayed away all night hunting and returned for me in the morning. She could sense the peace and calm that had moved over me in the night. And as a gesture of friendship she reached for my hand smiling with warmth and approval. But as her hand went out to meet mine, the old crone shrieked in alarm…

CHAPTER 4

The morning sunlight glared through my window as my alarm shrieked over and over. Slapping the snooze button I tried to return to my dream. When that wouldn't work, I tried to recall what the witch had said in my dream; words, phrases, anything solid. But when I couldn't remember anything of substance- I finally concluded that it was only a dream. I wouldn't learn anything new about myself from dreams and wishes. Kelly was right- the only way to learn more about being a banshee was through real life and getting my hands dirty.

Unfortunately, the one thing I did remember was the old woman repeating the phrase, "Don't trust her. Promise me you won't put your faith in the oldest evil on earth."

It took almost two years to warm up to Kelly, so it bothered me that my subconscious was still warning me off of her. But on the one hand- why not; after Kelly packed me like a sardine into that coffin, who wouldn't be leery... but the truth was I wanted to forget it and move on. It wasn't a good way to start that day off, and nothing bad had happened, it was only a dream. I was still alive and best friends with a vampire.

Kelly wasn't in her usual spot before the start of school; greeting me on the back steps before first period. We didn't have any classes together until homeroom which was fourth period, so it wasn't too strange that I didn't see her first thing. But later that day when she wasn't in home room either, I worried.

If it was anybody else, I would have gone to the bathroom and called them on my phone, but Kelly never carried a cell phone. I wasn't one hundred percent sure, but I thought Kelly could get in touch with anyone she wanted simply by using her mind. But where did that leave me, how would I get a hold of her? Could I call her home?

But when I really thought about calling Kelly's house, I was chicken. It would be fine if I called and Kelly picked up the phone. But if it was Marney or one of the other vampires that lived with Kelly who answered- I don't know what I would say. Kelly's 'guardian,' Marney made me break out in cold sweat thinking about her, let alone the idea of actually having a conversation with her.

Kelly kept Marney away from me for good reason. And in the past, I had only seen Marney on two separate occasions. Once when Marney showed up at school to pick Kelly up and the other time Marney was standing outside their house watching the world go by with fierce intensity. Both times I saw Marney, I got the distinct impression she was looking me over and sizing up how many pints of blood were in me. Marney probably glutted herself daily on the blood of unsuspecting homeless men and runaway boys. I was sure she didn't have any moral dilemmas about drinking human blood. Marney had a mix of cougar and vampire written all over her face in equal proportions that spelled out P-R-E-D-A-T-O-R. Just thinking about Marney made me want to crawl under the nearest rock.

After having second thoughts about calling Kelly's home I decided I wouldn't call her house unless she was gone for several days. Missing one day or not showing up for homeroom wasn't cause for alarm- yet. I was still a little self-conscious about going through with the banshee prank and wondered if Kelly had any misgivings about that night too. Maybe it was a coincidence that Kelly wasn't at school.

Still feeling weird about the previous night's prank; the terrified teenagers, trying to maintain control of my banshee abilities, being stuck in a coffin by Kelly, and having an out of body experience... it was a lot to digest. I was so lost in my own world that I didn't notice a girl sit down in the desk directly in front of me.

Melanie Walker turned around in the chair and said, "Your friend crossed the line last night and she's going to pay for it." Then she smiled grimly before storming off.

Melanie Walker was a cheerleader and one of the most popular girls in school. I didn't personally know her, but I was surprised that she would threaten Kelly... but of course she didn't know Kelly was a vampire. She couldn't have known- to my knowledge Kelly had only told one person.

So why was Melanie bent out of shape? Getting bent about being scared silly seemed extreme, but then again, she was the main recipient of Kelly's Halloween prank. Was there something going on between them? And what happened while I was stuck in that coffin?

As the day wore on- I wished Kelly was at school, so we could talk. It was strange for her to miss a day of school- so why that day? Was it possible that she was sick or hurt? Maybe she ate something bad. Maybe she was injured.

Worrying about things I didn't know anything about like vampire biology, worried me more. After school, I walked home unsure of what to do. Should I call Kelly's house? Maybe I should go to her house to find out what was going on. Worrying was making me irrational. Forget Marney, I was going over there.

Despite being bundled up, I shivered the whole way over to Kelly's house. The setting sun made the temperature drop, but the main reason for the ice in my veins was Marney. What if she was there and Kelly wasn't home? What if Marney pulled me inside and made a meal out of me? I reached the doorstep as the last horrible thought popped into my head.

Kelly's house stood on top of a bluff overlooking Lake Michigan. It was the only art deco stucco home in the whole neighborhood- and it looked like something out of a period drama on TV. The house had an eerie vibe as if time had stopped for it sometime in the 1930s. Even the lawn and trees surrounding the house were old and stuck in the Depression.

But the most ominous feature of the house was that there were no windows in the front. Instead there was only a line of thick glass privacy blocks running up the side of the door. And so someone standing on the outside, like me, couldn't see inside and could only imagine what went on in the inside of the house. Not being able to get even a peek of the inside made the house mysterious– and knowing that the house was inhabited by a coven of four vampires made it worse. Was the inside sparse or luxurious? How did they live? Of course, I would never find out since Kelly wouldn't let me inside. And I would never force the issue, not with Marney living in there like a wild animal that was only partially domesticated.

Might as well get it over with and knock… in for a penny, in for a pound.

My knuckles were feeble on the door. There was a doorbell to my left but I was afraid to push it in and really announce my presence. Fortunately, the door snapped opened and Kelly popped her head outside to my extreme relief.

"What are you doing here? What a surprise!"

A miserable voice called from inside the house, "Who's at the door Kelly?"

"A druggie," Kelly replied loudly.

"Huh," I said.

"SHHHHH," said Kelly as she closed the door behind herself.

Before the door closed shut, someone groaned in pain.

Kelly lighted on the sidewalk and grabbed my elbow gently, moving us down the street away from her house at high speed. Houses and street signs blurred as she ushered me in the direction of our favorite spot to talk indoors. She knew I was cold and hungry.

As Kelly opened the door to the coffee shop, I asked, "How do you know I'm hungry and freezing?"

She tapped her head and said, "You know the mind reading ability- besides you're shaking."

"I was scared."

She nodded as I grabbed the most isolated couch in Paradigm, a coffee shop on Eighth Street. It was quiet and dark as I huddled on the couch trying to get warm. The place was oddly empty and we had it almost exclusively to ourselves.

At the front counter Kelly put in our usual order- hot chocolate and a sandwich, before she selected something from the sweet case for me. I liked Kelly's surprises, she never picked wrong. And of course Kelly ordered her usual which was nothing, not even a glass of water. In the early days when we first met, Kelly would fiddle with drinks or food to make it appear like she was eating or drinking along with me, but after a few months of us being friends she had given up that pretense.

While I waited for Kelly to bring my drink, I stared dully at the empty stage. The last shafts of sunlight made spotlights through the spokes of the bicycles hanging from the ceiling. Shadows swayed keeping eerie time to the piped music; an apparition played a set for me.

"I am glad to see you, but DON'T EVER COME TO MY HOUSE AGAIN!"

It sounded like Kelly was shouting. I looked around the shop, but no one stirred in our direction. The loudest intonation was directly said inside my head. Her warning was solely for me.

Kelly set my sandwich on the coffee table in front of me, but my appetite was gone.

I stared at the tips of my boots; it was the first time Kelly was angry with me. I didn't want to look at her.

"I understand."

"NO," Kelly quickly lowered her speaking voice, "no, you don't understand. What if I wasn't there today and you met Marney alone? I can't guarantee you would be safe. Maybe with Marney, I would give you a fifty-fifty chance, because you're not her type and she might have her wits about her. She might decide that snatching you up would bring down a lot of attention… But if she was entertaining friends all bets would be off. She runs with a cruel crowd."

"Kelly, I'm sorry. And actually that very thing crossed my mind when I was at your front door. But I was worried about you."

"You were worried about me. You're joking right. That's sweet of you Sinead, but what could possibly happen to me? Remember you were the one who said I was an apex predator. No one defeats the mighty vampire."

"Yeah, I remember," I said. "I was worried because you weren't at school and because you pissed off Melanie Walker."

"How do you know that?"

"She told me."

"What? Wow- has she got some nerve!"

Oddly enough Kelly was amused. "And I thought maybe the message hadn't gotten through that thick girlie, cheerleader skull…"

"I'm lost- remember I was out for part of the night."

"Okay I will fill you in; but there isn't much to tell you actually. After you passed out, Melanie was still standing there petrified and wouldn't move. So with you out I needed to scare her. Needless to say I got her and lover boy moving."

"I see, sort of- actually I still don't know what happened. What's going on? Why are you being vague?"

"Okay- let me give you a little background to the evening. I knew where Melanie and her buddies would be, because they were going to a big Halloween party that everyone was invited to. I also knew what was happening in advance, because I was honing in on Melanie's mind for some time. Melanie had planned a very special Halloween night. She was dressed up in what she thought was a really cute costume, and I could tell by reading her mind that she wanted to impress a special guy."

Still puzzled, I waited for Kelly to go on. How come I didn't know about this party? Kelly was probably invited but not me.

"Well to make a long story short- you scared her pretty bad in front of her friends and she couldn't go to the party and make out with her new boyfriend. That's why she's so angry."

That didn't answer my questions, and why did Kelly look sheepish?

"Okay but why couldn't she go to the party after you scared her... did she fall and hit her head running out of the cemetery? What happened? She's obviously not dead."

After a long few seconds, Kelly whispered "she soiled her undergarments in front of her friends."

Kelly turned up her nose and her eyes became narrow slits filled with disdain. It was funny the way she put it delicately like she was telling a Victorian girlfriend.

I doubled over with laughter.

"You mean she crapped her pants?"

"Yes. Well, she um defecated into her costume from being so afraid of … you. That's why she wouldn't move when you were shrieking at her."

My face turned blue from laughing. Some of the other customers were looking at us, in a curious way. They wanted in on the joke.

When I managed to catch my breath, I said, "How did you get her to move?"

"Oh, in the usual way, I swooped out at her from above with my fangs hanging out at her. Something like that…" Kelly waved her right hand like it was nothing.

"And she pooped," I cut in.

"Again, yes, but she pooped because of *you*, not me. I didn't foresee that. I wouldn't have tried to get her moving if I knew what she was doing standing there."

Tears ran out of my eyes, I hurt myself laughing.

"Maybe she has stomach issues," said Kelly.

"Yeah I guess so," I was still snorting.

"After she had her accident, I thought it was probably a good thing that I stashed you away for a while. I didn't want her to come back and murder you."

"Oh Wow!" I said. "She would kill me if she found out it was me. She hates you now."

"Indeed," Kelly said with a raised eyebrow.

"Kelly- you were so quiet last night when you left… I was worried that I didn't give off a good scare. Is something wrong?"

"No- I wasn't upset; you exceeded my expectations. It was great fun last night. I thought you were going over what you experienced as a banshee and I wanted to give you some space to think and recover. Anyway- I needed to check in on Marney."

"Okay- I don't read minds or thoughts or even people's emotions very well. Normal people can't tell if someone is being honest or if they are being polite, and hiding their true feelings. I wasn't sure if you were somehow disappointed with the evening."

"No- not disappointed at all. It was riotous fun."

I took a few bites out of my sandwich and smiled at Kelly. She was always surprising me and she surprised me then with her kindness.

"So, why do you have a grudge against Melanie?"

"I don't have a grudge against her."

"Well, okay- why did you want to scare her?"

"Oh well that. She cheated in science class because she was going to fail and get kicked off the cheerleading squad."

"What did that have to do with you?"

"She didn't do the work on several dissection projects and when she saw that we had similar handwriting, she stole one of my assignments which was quite good and passed it off as one of her own."

"So why didn't you turn her in? I am sure Mr. Lopez would have believed you, especially with a little persuasion."

"I know, but I didn't want her to get kicked off the cheerleading squad. She's good at it and I think that is all she has in life."

"What do you mean by that?"

"I don't know how to explain it, but this is the only time she will be a big deal. In the future she has a nice house, a nice husband that is always gone, and a bunch of children she has to keep her husband coming home to her."

"So now you can tell the future?"

"No, but I've been around for a long time, and I can tell you what happened to a lot of my old school mates; for most of them, nothing exciting happened. Unless you call being housewives, laborers, and secretaries exciting. There were a few people that got further up the rung, but for the most part, people on the whole turn out quite average and lead boring lives. In Melanie's case, maybe she will turn out different, but she isn't the brightest bulb on the porch. And if I am right and this is her only time to shine- I don't want to be the one to take cheerleading away from her."

"Did you get a bad grade?"

"Yes, but that sort of thing doesn't matter. I only go to school because you're there and if you're worried about Marney's reaction, that's a non-issue. Marney pretends to be my guardian as a cover up for her agenda; she doesn't even know what the school we attend is called."

"So why did you really want to scare Melanie, then?"

"I don't know? To dissuade her from a life of cheating and crime- I guess. I wanted her to know that I was onto her... perhaps she will do her own work in the future. Maybe I was trying to motivate her to be something other than a conniving, stuck up cheerleader. I do try to care about the humans you know. She is my lab partner and all..."

"Alright- but how did she knew it was you?"

"I wasn't wearing my mask. I wanted her to know it was me. But I didn't want anyone to know who the mysterious banshee was."

I finished eating my sandwich; Kelly had ordered a piece of chocolate cake for me. I was pretty sure she read my mind about chocolate but I didn't complain.

"What about all the houses you toilet papered? Are you mad at your neighbors?"

"Umm, no, I saw that on a TV show and wanted to see if I could do it better..."

It was exactly as I had thought; Kelly got a lot of her best and worst ideas from watching television.

On the way home, I asked her, "so why didn't you come to school?"

"Marney was sick and I was taking care of her."

"You guys can get sick?"

"Yes, if we drink blood from people who are sick, we feel the same way they do. If we drink blood that is tainted with drugs or alcohol, we feel the same effects as the person who drank or used drugs. Marney and her friends held a haunted house at one of the clubs down in Milwaukee. Needless to say this club is notorious for drug use and where there are drugs, it covers up the casualties."

Kelly was uncomfortable talking about Marney and what she got up to with her friends. But this somehow explained why Kelly was hesitant to drink human blood, not only was it full of chemicals and preservatives; and tasted bad, but there was the risk of getting drunk or worse if the person had used drugs.

"That sounds scary," I said as the chocolate cake rolled around in my stomach. Fear made me want to soil my pants too. I was afraid of vampires.

"It is- but they wanted to get high," she shrugged. "Marney has been slumming it for at least fifty years. Her friends are the same way, they aren't exactly well thought of in the vampire world. They are pretty low class."

Kelly didn't talk about other vampires very often, most of the time she kept me ignorant because she thought it was best for me. Not only was she was protecting me from some very real threats from vampires, she was protecting me from living in fear all the time.

"Why do you live with Marney?"

"Oh that, well- she's the one who made me."

CHAPTER 5

The terrible rumors about Melanie started going around
school the day after our little prank in Wildwood. So it
wasn't surprising when Melanie didn't show up for school
the following Friday. It was embarrassing enough for her
after what really happened; but the rumors going around
school were actually worse than reality. And there wasn't
anything Melanie could do to save her reputation. The
only thing she could do was put some distance between
her and the unfortunate event. She would be embarrassed
for a while, but it would blow over with time- when the
other kids had some new even more shocking gossip to
spread around school.

I was relieved when Melanie didn't show up at
school. I was afraid that she might actually confront Kelly
like she confronted me in homeroom. That would be a
huge mistake. Kelly could do way more to a person then
scare the crap out of them. She could break a person from
the inside out in ways I couldn't even fathom. I wouldn't
wish a vampire on my worst enemy, and Melanie certainly
wasn't someone I considered an enemy. In fact, I felt a
little sorry for her because I was partly to blame for her
embarrassment.

As for Kelly, I think in her own weird way she
thought she was making a statement to Melanie about not
cheating, fair play, and the moral high road. It wouldn't be

until later on in our friendship that I would discover-humans and vampires have very different ideas about what is considered fair play.

Kelly was back at school that Friday and if anything bothered her, she didn't let on. Since she was back, I assumed Marney was better, but I didn't ask Kelly about it. Very early on, Kelly plainly let me know I should politely butt out of her business, unless she was comfortable sharing it with me. I was on a need to know basis as far as Kelly was concerned.

Besides not asking Kelly about her home life, I kept silent about Melanie Walker and Halloween night; because it was distasteful to Kelly. I was more worried about Kelly's living situation, when I found out she was living with an addict, I didn't pay much attention to a little bit of gossip at school.

There was one little thing that bothered me about Halloween night. And that was, in all the stories going around school, no one mentioned Kelly even though she was seen by several people that night. It was as if that little, but extremely significant detail about Kelly being there when Melanie was humiliated had been left out. I was pretty sure Kelly had manipulated the minds of the students to forget, so she wouldn't be implicated in the gruesome story being repeated around school. And it bothered me that Kelly could erase details, manipulate our minds, and basically rewrite history. But if Kelly had used her powers of suggestion to conveniently remove herself from the situation, I wasn't going to ask her about that either.

Melanie wasn't the only one who wanted to get as much time as possible between her and Halloween night. When the school bell finally rang signaling the end of the week, I was relieved to be going home and getting as far away from high school as possible.

The last remaining autumn leaves littered the streets and sidewalks as I walked home alone. Sometimes Kelly walked with me, but then she got occupied with Marney's condition and whereabouts, and couldn't spare the time. I wasn't sure what was going on, but Marney caused a lot of stress for Kelly.

Once I had gotten used to being friends with Kelly, I spent a lot of time thinking about what Marney was up to. It was one thing to be friends with a vampire I trusted, and a whole other thing to know she lived with a crazy, drug addicted, blood thirsty mentor. The idea that my best friend could be over her head with Marney, upset me a lot. I didn't want Kelly to get hurt.

Just the fact, that Marney still drank human blood had to be stressful for Kelly. Marney wasn't making any new vampires and so that had to mean there were bodies piling up somewhere. There aren't a lot of homeless people in Wisconsin that could simply disappear. That was one reason I couldn't figure out why Marney and Kelly lived in Wisconsin. I imagined that vampires liked hunting somewhere it was hot year round- where the streets were filled with homeless people that might not be noticed if a few went missing. Where did the people Marney drank from, come from? And another thing- did Kelly have to dispose of the empties? Sometimes I gave myself the willies.

"You're Kelly's friend."

Was this a question or a statement? I turned around to face the boy standing behind me. He was strangely familiar.

"How do you know Kelly?" I asked.

It always surprised me when other people mentioned Kelly's name, like when Melanie had the other day. Knowing Kelly was a vampire made me feel like we had some sort of special, exclusive friendship.

"I don't know her. But I know what she did to Melanie on Halloween and I'm a little surprised that you're her friend."

I gave him the stink eye.

"Hey, sorry I didn't mean it like that."

"Well- what do you mean?"

"I don't know... You're a nice person, I can't see you scaring the crap out of people. You can't imagine how humiliating and embarrassing it was for Melanie! What's your friend's problem anyway?"

Continuing to glare at the boy, I seethed inside, making snappy comebacks in my head. Let's see- my friend's a vampire, your girlfriend is a self-centered cheater. Kelly wanted to scare Melanie straight, but she probably won't get it... end of story. I don't see any problems here.

Instead I blurted out, "ahhh- you're Melanie's new boyfriend. Well, if you must know your girlfriend stole one of Kelly's dissection projects and put her name on it, because she didn't want to get booted off of the cheerleading squad for failing."

"What? ...Hmmm- Okay, but why go to the trouble of trying to embarrass her in front of everyone? That was mean. She could just turn Melanie in to the teacher for cheating."

I had to admit that on the surface, Kelly appeared to be one of those mean girls, the type that got off on being vindictive to other girls. There was probably no way I could explain what Kelly did in a way that would make her look good.

Suddenly- I wanted to explain the whole story him; starting with the differences between us and vampires. But there wasn't a clever way to explain the subtle differences in human and vampire thinking to him, while at the same time leaving out the most important detail, which was that Kelly was a vampire... And I wanted to tell him Kelly's theory- that all Melanie had in this life to look forward to was cheerleading and that Melanie's life would probably go downhill into painful obscurity starting right after high school. All this would be easy to explain if *only* he knew Kelly was a vampire to begin with.

This was a dead end conversation, and since I wasn't going to tell him my best friend was a vampire, I ended it. "You might want to ask Kelly. She would have a better answer than I do."

"Okay," he said. He stood there for a few moments. He was waiting in case I changed my mind and said something else.

I didn't.

"Well I have to go." But he didn't leave; he was still standing there trying to find something else to say to make the silence less ominous.

"By the way, my name is Martin and I am not Melanie's boyfriend," he added waiting for me to introduce myself.

I stared at him like a fool, before he took the hint that I lacked social graces. Then he walked across the street, went into a brown brick house and slammed the front door.

My eyes followed every movement, mocking the back of his head with a stare that said 'good riddance.' It was too bad he couldn't see with the back of his head. But when his front door slammed shut- I was jolted back into reality. Martin had the most beautiful, deep dark brown eyes I had ever seen. And I probably wouldn't get a second chance to get that close to them again. I pretty much screwed up my chances of ever talking to him again.

What could have been a great weekend rapidly careened off an invisible cliff into long and boring at that point. Besides scaring Martin away, I probably wouldn't see Kelly all weekend. I was still worried about her, but I took it very seriously about going over to her house to check up on her. I was warned to stay away. I knew that I couldn't handle Marney or her friends if I somehow found myself alone with them. If their idea of fun was setting up a haunted house in a rave club to lure drug addicts in so they could drink their blood, I could only imagine, what kind of fun they would have with me if I showed up on their doorstep. Did any newspaper delivery boys or girls scouts selling cookies ever disappear from our neighborhood?

I wouldn't tempt fate twice. Kelly was right; she was a big vampire girl and could take care of herself, I shouldn't be worried… but I was.

Not only was I worried, but I was bored and agitated too- there wasn't anything fun for me to do that weekend. I didn't even have homework to occupy the time. After two years of having a vampire for a best friend, I had forgotten how to do anything exciting on my own. And I felt sorry for myself because I was dying a slow death from boredom.

Moping around my bedroom, I stared out the window at the carpet of leaves that covered my backyard. Martin's house could be seen from my window too. Raking was all I could come up with, but it was something. Raking my backyard would give me an excuse to go outside and spy on Martin, while at the same time earning brownie points with my mom. Sometimes I scared myself with my own genius.

Pulling a rake full of dead leaves, I casually made a pile as close to our picket fence as possible, before sneaking a peek at Martin's house. I didn't want to look like I was spying on my neighbors, but after repeating the same steps a few times; even I knew my raking wasn't casual looking or natural. I was like a lone idiot trying to case Fort Knox.

I had seen other girls stalking boys since middle school, but when it came down to me doing the stalking, this was unfamiliar territory. I was under a magnifying glass pointed at the sun. Every time I minded my own business I was okay, but the second I faced Martin's house my heart thumped in my chest like a jackhammer.

I didn't have much experience with boys and crushes. There was Julian Giles in the fourth grade, we used to hold hands during recess, but otherwise my love life was nonexistent. Later there were a few boys I found cute in junior high and high school, but I never did anything about it. Frankly, I didn't do anything about having any girlfriends to hang out with either, until Kelly came into my life.

Part of my problem was overcoming my shyness; or maybe my biggest fear about getting close to people was that I would be rejected if they found out I was a banshee. Before Kelly came along I saw being a banshee as a major liability. But after becoming her friend, I found out there were other people like me that accepted me for who I was. And knowing someone else accepted me made me a little more willing to take chances with guys.

On the other hand, I was probably analyzing things too much and the truth was that in the past I was too lazy to maintain any meaningful relationships...

"BOO!"

I screamed, clutching my rake handle, about to go ninja on the ghost in my yard.

"I'm sorry I didn't mean to scare you, I thought you saw me there. I was waving at you from across the street."

"I'm okay; I didn't see you there." I was not okay, I just swallowed my heart. Since when did it hurt to breathe?

"Are you hungry?" Martin asked.

"No, why do you ask?" How could I be hungry after that?

"My mom wants to invite you over. And I felt bad about what I said earlier. It didn't go well. I shouldn't have accused you of things or said bad things about your friend."

"Umm- okay."

"Anyway- I wanted to know if you would come over to my house for some coffee or hot chocolate? My mom has been baking."

"Yeah- sure, I would love too."

I sat the rake up against the fence and followed him across the street, trying not to look like an awkward puppy following her boy.

A draft of warm, fragrant air hit my nose when Martin opened the back door. Clearly there was a baker living in Martin's house named mom. Coffee was brewing; cinnamon was browning on whatever was baking in the oven and the weekend went from gray back to great in an instant.

"Hi," a friendly voice greeted me, "and you are?"

"Sinead Smith, I live across the street there," I pointed to the back of my house that could be seen from Martin's living room window.

"Are you hungry Sinead, I have coffee ready and cinnamon rolls that will be coming out of the oven in about two minutes. They're homemade, not from a can."

"Sure, I will have a cinnamon roll, but no coffee please."

I was already shaking from being nervous; I hadn't been this close to a boy since the fourth grade.

"Would you like milk or tea instead?"

"Maybe some hot tea, if you have decaf, thank you," I said as I tried to keep my hands busy while waiting for something to do with them.

"Please sit down," said Martin's mom as she pulled a chair away from the counter for me.

When I sat down, she extended a warm hand and said, "I'm Alice Cross."

I shook her hand. A million little thoughts whizzing through my brain as I did, but I couldn't settle on any of them. Not only did I hope Martin liked me, but I hoped the same of Alice.

Alice set a plate in front of me with two frosted cinnamon rolls and put a large mug of tea next to it. With a glance at the stove timer, she made a quick exit and left us.

Martin sat at the end of the counter, watching and waiting for me to eat.

"Did you move here recently?" I asked.

"Yes, about two weeks ago."

"Oh- I guess I didn't see you in school," I replied playing with the edge of my plate.

"Well- I saw you and Kelly."

Hmm- I took a big bite of one of the cinnamon rolls hoping it would buy me a few seconds. I chewed slowly. I didn't know what to think about that. Was he interested in Kelly? Did he bring me over here to talk about her? She was a vampire and maybe he was under her spell too. I kept forgetting that normal humans couldn't resist her; only freaks like me had a strong aversion to her.

I thought we were done talking about Kelly. I didn't like talking about Kelly with anyone, even with my own mother. It was confusing to her that I was secretive about my best friend, but after a year or so my mom finally got over it. I didn't like how Martin wanted to talk about Kelly for other reasons, for one, if he liked Kelly that would be hard to deal with. She's my best friend and a vampire; I didn't want to fight with her over the same boys. And another thing- did I have a duty to warn guys away from her? She wasn't exactly typical girlfriend material… in fact, I wasn't even sure she liked guys. I know what she liked; blood. She was pretty one dimensional in that regard.

"Okay- what do you want to know about Kelly?" My voice had a hard edge that I didn't want to be there, but I was already jealous.

"Nothing- you told me what happened. I was surprised you were her friend that's all, she's kind of mean."

"What? That again!" I stammered choking on the gooey pieces stuck to the roof of my mouth.

"Don't you think that was a cruel trick to play on someone?"

"No. Didn't you hear me tell you that Melanie stole Kelly's dissection projects?"

"Yes, but that doesn't make sense at all. Her final grade must have taken a serious dive after losing that project grade. I know I'm in that class- those projects were worth a lot of points. I think Kelly told you Melanie stole her project, so you wouldn't think she was a jerk when it got around school, that she was mean to Melanie. Why didn't your friend just turn her in and have her grade restored, like a normal person?"

Because Kelly wasn't normal… but I couldn't tell him that she was a vampire. Or that as a vampire Kelly didn't care about grades. It was the truth that Melanie stole Kelly's project. And since grades weren't important to Kelly, and she didn't want Melanie punished by the teachers, she came up with this. Kelly's Halloween prank was her idea of *Scared Straight*.

"It's not about grades. There's a lot of things about Kelly that won't make sense to you. She's different. There are a lot of things about me that won't make sense to you, either" I said.

"Like making a leaf pile against a fence?"

"I was going to jump into that pile."

"Against a fence? I don't think so. You were spying on me."

My face was on fire; hopefully it wasn't bright red too. I wasn't a good liar. But this was better than talking about Kelly.

"Ha! I knew it! It's okay- I understand. Spying on the new kid," Martin laughed.

I was barely breathing; Martin made me feel like I was on a hot plate. There was a small battle inside me that went back and forth between wanting to be near him and running insanely from his house.

"Ok, so what about you wouldn't make sense?"

"Umm… I don't know, when I think of something, I'll let you know," I said.

I was going for an air of mystery, but what I said came out sounding dumb. Thank God people aren't video recorded in real life. If I was the star of a reality show, it would be lame.

"I'm intrigued," Martin said lifting one eyebrow.

Obviously, I wasn't scaring him off. Was the temperature in his kitchen ninety degrees?

"I have to leave," I said, "my mom is probably wondering where I disappeared to and I have a lot of things to do tonight."

"Like what?"

I dropped some of the sticky, cinnamon roll onto my plate. I wasn't sure what to say because I was lying. I didn't have anything to do all weekend.

"You have some frosting on your face," Martin said.

"Where?"

"Here," he said rubbing it off my chin gently with his thumb.

I ducked my head out of the way in case he was about to do something else. On TV this is the part where the couple violently kisses for the first time, on my reality TV show this was the part where I run.

The last thing I heard as I slammed the back door of his house was, "hey- I won't bite…"

87

My heart was thumping in my chest when I slammed the back door to my house. My mom was standing in the kitchen and she gave me a weird look, "you alright Sinead? I've been looking for you."

"Yeah, I'm fine why?"

"Kelly called and I didn't know where you were. I tried to call you, but you left your cell phone on your desk."

"Kelly called the house."

"Yes - you are best friends aren't you?"

I could tell she still wanted to ask me things about Kelly. There were always unanswered questions that I couldn't answer even for her. The best thing about my mom was that she never pried, just trusted that I was basically good and stayed out of my business.

"Yeah, sure it's just that... oh never mind," I said.

There was nothing for me to explain to my mom. I could always end all the hanging questions with three simple words, *Kelly's a vampire*. Sure maybe that would answer everything, but only if you believed.

Upstairs in my room, I grabbed my cell phone that no one ever called and looked at the call records. There was a call on my phone too, from a local number, but no message. Putting the phone within reaching distance, I sat down at my desk and waited for Kelly to call back. I waited and waited and waited... after about an hour of waiting, I realized the time would pass faster if I actually did something, instead of staring at my phone for a call that may never come.

As I started down the stairs to watch a movie, the house phone rang. I almost tripped down the whole flight of stairs to get to it.

"Got it Mom," I yelled without checking the caller id.

"Hello," I said.

"Hi Sinead, it's Kelly, can I come over?"

"Yeah- of course, I'm not busy."

"Okay but I am going to come in through the upstairs, I don't want your mom to know I'm coming over."

"Are you okay?"

"Yes, wait for me upstairs in your room with the lights off okay? I'll be there shortly."

Something was wrong; I could tell from the way Kelly's voice strained. I put the phone back in the cradle and went back to my room.

Upstairs- I closed the door, turned off the light, and sat on my bed. When I couldn't sit still for another second I got up and fidgeted with the curtains. I peeked outside, nothing but a cloudless sky. I opened the window and stuck my head out for a better look. The room filled with November air and before I could shut the window, Kelly lighted into the room.

The minute Kelly hit the carpet; I shrieked without warning. In an instant, Kelly was on me. She grabbed my face and held my mouth clenched shut and then pinned my body to the floor in one swift move. Kelly had me down and incapacitated before I had a chance to figure out what was going on. That old familiar sickening, buzzing noise filled my ears and I convulsed wildly on the floor. If Kelly wasn't there to hold me down I would have flown out the window whether or not it was open and crashed to the ground below.

"Breathe," she whispered through clenched teeth.

Instinctively, I knew it took Kelly every ounce of her power to keep me from flying out the window. And I struggled to calm down and relax for her sake too. My mouth was clenched shut under her right hand, but she had uncovered my nose. I breathed in and out as hard as I could through my open nostrils.

My heart banged into my ribcage, while I struggled for oxygen. I was in the middle of a full blown shriek, and going banshee; who died? Could it be Kelly? But she was already dead. How could Kelly set me off? Something was obviously wrong with her. I needed to get my head back together and get calm fast. I listened to the sound of my breath, trying to meditate on it, but it didn't stop the urge to scream.

Then I remembered- my breathing didn't matter. Had her heart stopped? Could Kelly be dying all over again? When Kelly carried me back home the first time I turned into a banshee in front of her, I felt how different she was. Kelly was cold and her chest barely moved when she breathed. The way she felt alive was certainly different. But her heart beat was strong from the blood of whatever animals she had drank earlier that night.

My left arm was going numb from being pinned under me by Kelly. I pried my arm out from under my back, nearly wrenching it out of my socket. And when I did get my arm free, it was so numb that I could hardly move it towards my target- her heart. After a few seconds my hand found its mark on her icy chest and felt for her heartbeat. I held my fingertips there, pressed up against the cavity above her left breast. Instead of a deep thrumming, I felt nothing.

"I'm still alive," she said as she pulled my hand up to her carotid artery so I could feel a faint pulse.

Finally, my fingertips met a small tiny rhythmic tremor that I knew was her heartbeat, only completely devoid of blood. Something was wrong with Kelly. She was a hollowed out husk. It took a few moments of feeling her vampire heart, before something inside of me switched off and registered Kelly as fully alive.

Kelly loosened her grip on me when my breathing became natural and less labored. The buzzing in my head had subsided and was almost gone. After a few more minutes of resting on the floor, Kelly helped me into a sitting position. I felt like I was hit by a truck. I was always so disorientated and drained when I became a banshee. And this frightened me- I wasn't in control again. Just when I thought I had made some headway on

Halloween. This had to get easier. I wouldn't be a child sheltered from death for long.

Upright and sitting on my own, I took a deep breath. Something was horribly wrong with Kelly. She was always naturally cold and white, but that night she was more so. The light from outside illuminated her pale face and accentuated the dark circles under her eyes. Kelly was more of a drained corpse, and less a vampire. And there was a dark spot on her shirt under her right collar bone that appeared to be blood.

My first thought was that she had drunk blood from a human and it went terribly wrong. I was afraid to ask though, because her answer could change everything.

Finally, I said what was on my mind, "Did you kill someone tonight?"

"No."

She stared at the carpet as if she wasn't telling the truth or maybe hiding something.

"It was nothing like that. I need some time to rest and think. Just a few minutes, Sinead, I don't want to be alone right now. I'll leave soon; I need to hunt... animals."

Kelly was still making it clear her position on drinking humans with me. She knew how much it disturbed me to think of her latched on to someone and drinking their blood, but was it the truth? Something was wrong; Kelly was clearly shaken and *thirsty*. What had happened?

My eyes settled on the two angry red marks above her collar bone.

"What happened, who did this to you?"

I reached out to touch her neck, to expose the damage half hidden under her T-shirt collar.

Shocked, I cried out in pain as she slapped my hand away. Before I could react she jumped towards the window to take flight.

"I am so sorry Sinead. I didn't mean to hit you. Don't! You can't touch my blood if I am wounded. I'm sorry if I hurt you, I wasn't thinking when I came…," she trailed off and opened the window again, this time to leave.

"Don't go," I said, "I'm okay- you were only trying to protect me from doing something stupid. I should have known better. Will you tell me what happened? Where are you going?"

"I shouldn't tell you anything, for your sake, but I can't go home for a while. I didn't know where to go. I didn't want to be alone."

"Marney did this?"

Kelly put a single finger to her lips. She shook her head to warn me not to say anything further.

I acknowledged her but repeated my questions, "Where are you going? When will I see you?"

"I don't know- soon. I need to hunt and rest. It's not good for me to be around you in this condition. Please forgive me. When things are different... and better, I'll be back. I promise."

As quickly as she came, she was gone. The curtains fluttered briefly and my bedroom was filled with cold air. I closed my window, but not the curtains and pressed my face to the glass. For a long time I stared out into the night lost in dark thoughts.

I knew she had left to hunt first, because she needed to eat, but where would she go after? Normally, I didn't want to know anything about her eating habits, but this time I wished I could follow her to make sure everything would be all right again.

Too tired to stand for much longer staring out the window, I got into bed and huddled under the covers. After an hour or so passed, my bedroom door opened. I closed my eyes and pretended to sleep. I could sense what I couldn't see. My mom stood in the door wondering if I was really asleep or if I wanted to talk.

I wasn't exactly sure how mother's intuition worked, but my mother had a lot of it. Even if she didn't know what was going on with Kelly or me, she had a sixth sense about me. And it comforted me that she was concerned, even if I couldn't talk to her about it.

CHAPTER 6

My mother stared at me in the dark. Her eyes burned into me; did she know I was a banshee? Would she stop loving me now that she knew I was different?

It was strange, how I could feel her presence in the dark. She wouldn't go away, even though I pretended to sleep. Her eyes burned through me with an emotion I didn't understand. It wasn't quite anger. Was it disgust, or even hatred? What was written all over her face? Her face pressed against glass and distorted. In a daze, I rushed over to the window to open it. She was outside my bedroom clinging to the ledge.

Marney was staring at me like I was a caged animal in a zoo, her face a combination of rage and thirst!

I screamed- a normal scream that brought my mom running into my bedroom.

"Are you all right?"

"Yeah, I just had a really intense nightmare," I said. At least I hoped it was a nightmare, I wasn't sure if Marney wasn't outside my window clinging to the siding like a giant spider. I was too afraid to check.

"Want to talk about it?"

"Ummm- no," I said quickly.

My mom sat at the foot of the bed, reassuring me with the gentle pressure of her hand on my calf.

"I'm getting up to watch TV," I said. Huddled in my blanket, I went downstairs and turned on the cable box. Flipping through the channel menu, I noticed a lot of late night movies were horror movies.

"Would you like me to stay with you?" My mom asked.

"Yeah, I would like that."

My mom sat down beside me and we watched old movies until the sun came up.

I slept all day Saturday. By Sunday, Martin was erased from my mind, from worrying about Kelly and being terrified of Marney. My mind jumped back and forth between the two vampires, unable to settle on either and I was filled with gut wrenching anxiety. Kelly had led me to believe that vampires were invincible, but I was beginning to believe otherwise.

The only thing that really mattered was that Kelly kept her promise to come back soon. I didn't want to admit it at the time, but with Kelly gone I didn't have a lot to look forward to. I had gotten used to her making my world more colorful and exciting. Without her- life was kind of bland.

On Monday Kelly wasn't at school, but I wasn't expecting her to show up. My gut feeling was that she was okay, or at least away from Marney and that made me feel better.

The day dragged, school was an endless stream of questions and assignments. It was one thing to dread school, and another thing to dread the future. I couldn't shake the feeling that things had hopelessly fallen apart ever since Halloween night, when Kelly decided to prank Melanie Walker and dazzle the neighborhood with her magic skills. I knew she didn't mean any harm, but everything had changed since and the scales were tipped against us. We would have to be on guard, because the days of carefree adventure were over.

At lunch time, I sat in a back hallway eating a sandwich, a book propped in my lap. It was the way I spent most of my lunches before I met Kelly, alone and buried in a book. I tried to get into reading, but my mind kept wandering away from the words.

A shadow crossed the page and sat down on the steps above me. "Hi," said Martin.

"Hi," I said back. I wasn't the best conversationalist.

"What are you reading?"

"A book about Celtic mythology- stories about ancient gods and things."

"Things? Hmm…Is it good?"

"Yes."

"I didn't see you around this weekend. You never did jump into your pile of leaves." He was smiling.

"No, I didn't. I had a lot of things to do on the weekend." Was he spying on me?

Martin's left eyebrow curled up, but before he could interrogate me about the weekend, the bell rang. There was five minutes to get to class.

"I guess I will see you later," he said.

My heart thumped in my chest and my stomach did somersaults when he left. Why couldn't I be nice? Why didn't I show a little interest? I couldn't blame him for taking off when the bell rang; I barely said one civil word.

It was that time of year when half the student body happily paired off. Couples were hugging and kissing and engaging in all sorts of obnoxious displays in the halls. It was making me sick to watch and by Tuesday, I really did get sick. But I couldn't blame the other students; the truth was- I was making myself sick. Worrying and anxiety dragged me down and I went home after the school nurse put in a call to my mom to pick me up early.

For three days, I slept and barely ate. Sleep was anything but restful, because I immediately fell into vivid, anxious dreams with the major characters alternating between Kelly, Martin, and Marney. Unfortunately, most of the time I picked Marney to be the main player in the dramas acted out in my feverish subconscious.

That Friday morning, I was more than ready to go back to school. Being sick at home was not fun. I was tired of running from Marney in my nightmares. At least at school, I had to try and stay awake; and when I was awake I wasn't being chased by vampires. And another benefit of going back to school was that I would be surrounded by friendly faces. But when I got to school Martin was absent and Kelly was still gone too.

After school I was surprised by Kelly standing behind the garage waiting for me. I would have walked right into my house without noticing her if I hadn't heard the light crunch of leaves as she walked around the corner to greet me.

She looked good; her skin a healthier shade of antique white and the dark circles under her eyes had faded. From a distance, the two angry holes on her neck had scabbed over and could be mistaken for a pair of matching dark freckles. Best of all, she had a serene look on her face as if she hadn't a care in the world.

I dropped my backpack and hugged her. Kelly didn't flinch or resist me, but it was like hugging a marble column with arms. She wore a slight smile and gave me a small squeeze back before shoving me away gently.

"Can I buy you a sandwich?"

"Yes, let me tell my mom where I am going, and we can leave," I replied.

I had a million questions I wanted to ask Kelly even though she was gone a short time. And as we walked I accumulated more questions with each step, but only one was important.

"Are you back at home with…?"

I trailed off to avoid saying Marney's name out loud. It felt like I was invoking a curse. It was as if I said her name out loud, she could hone in on me at any time and find me. I felt like a kid in a bathroom mirror playing Bloody Mary…

Marney, Marney, Marney! Because I said her name three times- now She COULD GET ME!

CRUNCH!

Kelly crushed an acorn hidden underneath the leaves and I jumped. I was nervous and on edge- and if Kelly hadn't noticed before, she knew it then.

Kelly put her hand on my arm and said, "No and that's what I want to talk to you about. I'm not going back home, Sinead. I can't live with Marney anymore. Anyway- she's moving down south soon and I don't want to go with her. She doesn't want to spend another winter in Wisconsin."

"She's leaving. You mean to Phoenix or Florida."

"No further south to South America, maybe Columbia."

"What?"

"Marney and her friends have a taste for cocaine after the haunted house."

Cocaine! That would somehow explain Marney's unpredictable behavior after Halloween.

When we reached Paradigm, Kelly opened the door to heaven, the smell of coffee and baked goods nudging me back towards blissful contentment for the first time in days.

"Why can't you stay in your house and she leave." I asked sinking into a patterned sofa in the back, watching the steam curl off of my coffee mug.

"Marney doesn't want to go without me. And she'll be looking for me soon. I've left to hunt before, but I've never been gone this long. When she figures out I'm not coming back, she'll go looking for me. For all I know she's after me right now. After what she did, I am pretty sure Marney knows I am not coming back."

I shuddered, "Could she find you here- right now?"

"Yes, if I stay long. I need to leave right away and get plenty of distance between her and I. That's the only way for me to get away from Marney for good. If I don't-she will ambush me and make me go with them. But Marney will eventually tire of looking for me and leave. Her friends are ready to go. They want to move on to where the people and drugs are."

"How can she make you leave with her?"

"I'd rather not speculate, but there are three of them and one of me. I'm sure together the three of them could make me do anything Marney wants me to do, if they get a hold of me."

"I don't understand why she wants you to come with her?"

"It's hard to explain, but she needs a handler and she trusts me. Marney doesn't trust her friends. She can't- they're addicts too, looking for the next thrill and they're not exactly very discreet anymore. Hosting a haunted house at one of the biggest raver clubs in Milwaukee isn't exactly flying under the radar.

"Being dependent on blood is bad enough. But being addicted to alcohol and drugs on top of the thirst is incapacitating- then you need both to survive. They need blood with drugs in it to maintain their sanity. But the effects are short lived and vampires like Marney are unpredictable and out of control. She puts us at risk to vampire hunters on a regular basis. There aren't many vampires who would be sad if Marney disappeared off the planet."

"Vampire hunters?"

"Yes, like the fictional Van Helsing- the vampire hunter that hunted Dracula. There are real vampire hunters out there looking for us and they're dangerous. The hunters have tricks to keep vampires unaware they are being tracked. Right now, there are about a half a dozen vampire hunters in the world that I'm aware of and they are very good at what they do. The hunters kill at least two dozen vampires a year, maybe more."

My blood ran cold- Kelly really wasn't as invincible as I once thought. Her world was lonely and dangerous.

"So besides Marney coming after you, do you think there could be a vampire hunter after you right now?"

"No- but I would be the last to know. That was one of the reasons we relocated to Wisconsin; vampire hunters track us by our eating habits. Most vampires aren't located in the north. Vampires go where the food is, like following a herd. Homeless people don't generally live in cold climates, but you already know that."

"So why is Marney here, if there aren't a lot of available people?"

"Drugs and safety- Marney came here because Milwaukee is a legendary for beer and being a party town. There's a group of vampires that live comfortably in Chicago, because of the huge population of homeless people living in abandoned buildings, but not so much up here. And since there aren't many vampires past Chicago, Marney thought it would be a good place to set up shop. She doesn't like to be around other vampires- besides her lackeys.

"By coming up here she pretty much insured we would be left alone. It hasn't worked out though. Even with Milwaukee and Green Bay, there isn't a huge supply of human prey that won't be noticed if they go missing. And now that it's cold, most homeless, transient people are in shelters or have moved south. For me it doesn't matter, whether its summer or winter, there's plenty of wild animals up here for me to live on. But for Marney and her crew last winter was rough. They spent most of the winter drinking homemade Bloody Marys and waiting for the snow to melt. They don't want to spend another winter here."

"Bloody Marys?" I had heard of the cocktail, but I wasn't sure if that was what she meant.

"Yes, it's a vampire cocktail... blood and vodka or blood and beer or blood and well pretty much anything alcoholic...just substitute blood for tomato juice, add alcohol and stir. You've never heard of a Bloody Mary?"

"Not that kind." I choked; my coffee went down the wrong pipe, "Gross, where do they get the blood from?"

"They steal it from the blood bank. It's quite pathetic, I know, but I only take blood that is about to expire."

"That's awful. What? Why do they make you steal the blood?"

"Actually I volunteered to do it, so I can make sure the blood that I take is expiring and about to be incinerated. Besides if Marney or her friends were let loose in a blood bank, they would bring a lot of attention down on us. They don't have a lot of self-control. When I handle things for Marney, things are a lot neater, a lot tidier. When Marney takes care of things, everything goes haywire. Believe me- I know this from personal experience."

"So I guess you are leaving today?"

"Yes, but I will be back soon. I promised you a lot of things before this happened and I haven't forgotten. We still have a trip to take. Keep thinking about all the plans we made and before you know it this will be a thing of the past. This will be old news."

"We weren't going to leave until after I graduate next year. You aren't going to be gone that long are you?"

"No- Marney will get tired of looking for me soon enough and her friends will get her moving. And once she is in South America, doing her own thing she won't want me back. She won't even care about me anymore."

"How can you be so sure? What makes you think she won't want you back if she trusts you, if she needs you so much?"

"Because I am not her only protégé and I won't be her last. I'm not anything special to her anymore- Sinead. She has had several besides me and she can always make more vampires if she wants to. A part of me wants her to make a new vampire, so she will move on and leave me alone. But God forbid she makes another vampire. A vampire protégé of Marney's is someone to be pitied."

The BLT that Kelly ordered for me crumbled like sawdust in my mouth, despite liberal dollops of mayonnaise and a tomato keeping it moist. There was nothing I could do about Kelly leaving; I just hoped she would come back for me. What if she forgot me?

"What happened to the other vampires Marney made? You said there were more."

"You don't need to know the details- it was very bad for them."

"No- Kelly, don't be vague with me now. You have always told me the truth. What happened?"

"It's simple; when she was tired of them or didn't trust them anymore she killed them."

"So you lied to me, when you said they might kidnap you and force you to go? You didn't want me to know that Marney might kill you?"

"That's a little strong Sinead; I doubt Marney wants to kill me. She would rather try to force me to come with her. But she is very unpredictable and she turned on me before. I could be wrong and she is out for my blood, but somehow I don't think I have crossed a line with her yet, but that doesn't mean I want to find out. I have a lot more living to do and I don't plan on doing it in South America babysitting Marney."

"Should I be afraid of Marney once you are gone?"

"Yes... I mean no, don't worry. I made sure you are protected, so I wouldn't worry excessively. But I don't want you to put yourself at risk either."

"What did you do to protect me?"

"I can't tell you specifics Sinead, but I promise I have taken care of that. You will be safe while I am gone. Marney will leave the area in a week or two, and in the meantime I am going to give you a set of rules to use for the next month or so. Please listen to me carefully.

"Don't walk anywhere alone, at least for the next month. Under no circumstances should you go to my old house, no matter what. If Marney does try to contact you by telephone or in person, do not respond to her in any way, even if she says I am in the area or that she knows something about me. Even if you think I am back, but you haven't actually seen me or spoken to me, don't go to her. And don't try to find out if I am back on your own. I promise you will know when I am back and when it's safe."

"Okay," I sniffled a little and tried to pretend it was from being sick the past few days. But it was a losing battle, when I tried to hold in the tears that rolled out of the sides of my eyes. I was tired, scared, and overwhelmed. I went three steps back to the same emotional state I was in before Kelly showed up and brought me to the coffee shop. Or maybe it was worse; I was frightened more after we talked.

"It's going to be okay, Sinead. Nothing is going to happen to me or to you. I promise. This is just a little inconvenient for both of us right now. I'm going to leave now, but I will be back soon."

"Wait, you're leaving right now? But…"

Kelly squeezed my hand hard and flew out the back door of the coffee shop, into the co-op that was in back. Long goodbyes made Kelly uncomfortable- maybe as uncomfortable as I felt about being unceremoniously dumped by my best friend. My best friend who happened to be my only safety net against other vampires; basically just told me to 'stay safe,' and left.

As soon as I realized the severity of Kelly leaving, I jumped up and tried to follow her. I ran into the co-op but found it empty besides the store clerk leaning over the counter reading *Mother Earth News*. Running out the door, I scanned both sides of the street for Kelly but the streets were empty.

"Did you see which way the girl with long black hair went?" I asked the clerk when I returned inside.

"What girl? No one's been in here the last hour."

I walked back into Paradigm, where our waitress stood by the co-op entrance waiting for me.

"Oh sorry," I said flustered, "I didn't mean to leave without paying. I was running after my friend. I forgot to say something to her."

"Oh no, your friend already paid your bill. Don't worry about that. Here- she told me to give this to you." The waitress pulled out an envelope from the inside of her half apron and handed it to me.

"Thank you."

"Would you like a refill?" She asked.

"Yeah, might as well."

The barista brought me a refill, while I examined the envelope. The outside front read in Kelly's distinctive Edwardian script.

To Sinead: Open in Case of an Emergency

I turned the envelope over and broke the seal on the gummed flap. This wasn't an emergency, but I had to know what she had left me with. But what if it was a one-time thing and I ruined it by opening it... I handled the envelope gingerly as if it was filled with a protective charm.

Too bad if it only worked once, I ripped open the envelope. Inside was a slip of paper with a phone number and name on it; *Rex*. Kelly left me a phone number? I wasn't safe anymore.

I pulled out my cellphone and dialed my house. When a voice picked up the other end, I said into the phone, "Mom will you come get me? I'm at Paradigm."

"Sure, are you feeling okay? That's a long walk, for someone who's been sick. I'll be there in about fifteen minutes. Don't walk home."

"Thanks Mom," I ended the call, tucked Kelly's envelope into my pocket and waited for my mom to arrive. At least someone cared about me.

CHAPTER 7

After my mom drove me home, I hid in my basement as if it was a fallout shelter from vampires. There I spent most of that weekend alternating between watching movies and playing video games on the computer. Only once in a while, did I go upstairs for food or drink, but only when I got tired of listening to my stomach making loud, angry noises to get my attention. Fortunately, I was sick the week before so my mom didn't think I was acting any stranger than usual and she left me alone.

The following Monday my mom drove me to school in the morning and I easily convinced her to drop me off and pick me up in the afternoons as well, since it was November. I wasn't going to take any chances and walk to or from school alone. It would be stupid of me to not follow Kelly's instructions, even if I was upset with her.

The first couple of weeks after Kelly left went by uneventfully; nothing unusual happened at school or anywhere else for that matter. I don't know what I expected, but I was keyed up and on red alert at all times for strange, creepy pale people following me.

Being scared all the time was like throwing water on a fire when it came to Martin. All the excitement I felt when we first met dissipated. I was so preoccupied with looking out for vampires- that every time I saw Martin, I never said much more than 'hi' or 'bye' to him.

November had almost disappeared from the calendar and I felt somewhat better. I had convinced myself, that a few more weeks of waiting for Kelly to return wouldn't be difficult and that she would be back by Christmas. And if we were lucky, Marney was already packed and ready to leave, if she hadn't left already. I was anxious to find out if Marney had left town, but I wasn't going to risk my life to walk past Kelly's old house to look for signs of vacancy.

At the beginning of Thanksgiving week, I woke to an early blizzard and school was canceled. The streets and sidewalks were still under plowed that Tuesday so I spent another day at home watching cars go by from my upstairs window. Wednesday was a half day for Thanksgiving break, and my mom turned up again at school to bring me home at noon.

Thanksgiving kept me occupied with something to do besides homework and hiding out from the neighborhood vampires. For the first time in weeks, I stopped thinking about Marney for more than an hour at a stretch and my appetite was back.

When the Thanksgiving prayer was said at our table, I mumbled a few words out loud about being thankful for the food. Then I made a silent petition for

Kelly's safe return so we could go back to our lives prior to this mess. Mulling over our situation I hoped that Marney had moved on without Kelly. It wasn't just that I was bored without Kelly; I was worried about her safety too.

For the first time in weeks, I tasted food not sawdust. And the rest of Thanksgiving break went by in a fog- I spent those four days in a turkey laced coma grateful that it was boring. And by Sunday night, I was ready to go back to school and craving school hot lunches. I was sick of eating variations of turkey and hoped that my mom wouldn't get creative with turkey leftovers and pack me a lunch.

The snow plow trucks worked hard over the weekend pushing and clearing snow. Early Monday morning after Thanksgiving, I was dropped off at the front door of school and handed an ominous looking lunch sack. But even the greasy paper bag wouldn't crush my spirit and I tossed the last of turkey carcass sandwich in the first available trash can. I was confident that Kelly and I would be back to hanging out again soon.

And since my appetite returned, I started eating lunch in the cafeteria, instead of tucked away in a back hallway with my nose in a book. I even sat with Martin and a group of his friends in the lunchroom. Martin had made a few friends by then and it felt nice to be included in a group for once. As the days passed, I was less self-

conscious and joked with Martin's friends and flirted a
little bit with Martin during lunch.

My mom continued chauffeuring me back and forth to
school and then another Saturday came, this one marking
the beginning of December.

Outside it was cold and snowy and houses
everywhere had Christmas lights up. Our tree was up too
and Christmas was around the corner. In another week or
so perhaps Kelly would be back and knocking on the back
door of my house.

It had been about a month since Kelly had left, and
I was no longer worried about Marney or any other
vampires. From time to time- I wished I knew for sure if
Kelly was happy and safe wherever she was. And I tried to
picture what she was doing at the exact moment I thought
of her.

Oddly enough, sometimes when I felt lonely, I
tried to remember what it felt like when Kelly was in my
head reading my thoughts. It was strange that I would
miss her reading my mind, when in the very beginning-
when I first met her it made me sick to my stomach to
have her inside my head. But I had long moved on from
being disgusted by Kelly. And the truth was there was a
time when I used to feel comforted when I could sense her
in my head alongside me.

I can't explain it, but having someone else inside
your mind finally closes the door on that big question: 'am

I alone in the world?' It was one of the few times that I knew I wasn't a small insignificant dot alone in a vast universe.

December was vanishing too and Kelly still hadn't returned to Sheboygan. I was certain that Marney was long gone from our small city on the lake. There were no newspaper reports of missing people or mass break-ins at the blood bank, so I assumed Marney and her buddies had left the area quietly and without inflicting some last bit of damage before leaving.

      Christmas was almost here and I still hadn't heard anything from Kelly- not a phone call, or email, not even a short text to let me know she was still *alive*. The dark days of early winter were long and abstract. I was starting to lose some of my optimism as winter unfolded and dark thoughts crossed my mind. I was worried and depressed again. I felt safe from Marney but frightened for another reason- maybe Kelly had moved on without me. Kelly was gone so long, that I often thought she had forgotten me and wasn't coming back. Why would she? Sheboygan was dark and cold in the winter and nothing exciting ever happened here, aside from her. There was a whole new world out there for her since she had broken free of Marney.

      The only thing for her here was me and I wasn't sure our friendship was enough to bring her back. Kelly was an old, adventurous soul compared to me. I was still a wall flower and not much of a friend when it came to stirring up the excitement we both craved. I couldn't even attract a boyfriend; much less maintain a few friendships with anyone else beyond what she and I had. It wouldn't surprise me if she lost interest in me and it hurt me to think we might not be friends in the future.

Suddenly the most excitement in my life went from avoiding vampires to keeping my English assignment partners focused on a group project and not on what they were getting for Christmas. Getting my group to do any work was like pulling teeth and my mom would care if my grade suffered. To get the work done, I stayed late at school to do the *group* assignment by myself.

After one really long afternoon of trying to piece together notes from my absent partners, I forgot to call my mom for a last minute ride home. When I finally took out my cell phone to call her, there was only a small sliver of day light left.

All the vampires that had haunted me were a million miles away drinking blood and staying warm. My world was filled with cold, comfortable boredom and was entirely too safe again. Putting away my phone, I decided to walk home to get some fresh air and take a break from due dates and feeling used.

I was a few feet out the front door of school, when I stopped dead in my tracks. At the end of the block, Martin was talking to a girl. A dry spot formed in my throat as I watched. All of my jealous wiring was electrified. What were they talking about?

I should have stopped gawking at them and walked home but my feet wouldn't cooperate with common sense. I was glued to the spot. While still cemented to the top step, I watched as the girl whispered in Martin's ear while touching his forearm. It jolted me with another strong pang of jealousy.

I waved at Martin to break up the tension, but he didn't acknowledge me. Maybe he really didn't see me, but I was sure the girl knew I was watching them. And as if reading my mind, she looked over at me before leaving Martin. After a few seconds, Martin turned towards me too for a brief instant. Expecting him to wave at me or something, instead he ignored me again and turned in the opposite direction to follow after her.

"Wait," I yelled, confused as to why he would ignore me. I wanted to yell at Martin a second time, but I kept my mouth shut when I noticed the two freshman girls below me on the steps.

The girl had already disappeared around the block and Martin followed her at high speed. Hitting the sidewalk as fast I could, I tried to catch up to him, but the shoes I wore were not made for snow and had little traction. Although the sidewalks had been shoveled, there were plenty of patches of ice and slush to slow me down. The more carefully I walked to avoid slush minefields and falling on my butt, the faster he walked away. After following Martin for about three blocks, he was so far ahead I couldn't see him anymore.

Was he deliberately avoiding me? Maybe he didn't want me to ask him about the girl. I had pushed him away for so long, he probably thought I wasn't interested. And now even if he thought I was interested, it wouldn't matter. He had obviously moved on.

I reached North Fifteenth Street and saw Martin up ahead again with his head down and moving fast. But instead of turning up the street that led to our neighborhood, Martin turned right and walked into a dead end street. I was nervous as I continued following him. Maybe he was going to a friend's house do homework. It would be embarrassing if he caught me following him like a crazy stalker.

Crossing the street; I saw the girl again out of the corner of my eye. My heart sunk into the pit of my stomach, Martin was following her. I paused briefly to make a note of the house she went into. It was a brick house at the far end of the block. Then I waited until they were both out of sight before I turned into the dead end too so I could memorize the house numbers.

I don't know why I followed Martin up the block like a lovesick fool. I had almost forgotten that I had feelings for him, until I saw him with another girl. And it triggered all these emotions I had stuffed down inside of me while I was obsessed with vampires. With my brain in overdrive, I tried desperately to tell myself that nothing was going on. Martin obviously had a class with this girl and they were going to do homework together.

The air was extremely cold and the sun almost down. I slunk backwards out of the cul-de-sac, embarrassed. When I turned around, I walked right into a tall, greasy man coming out of the Silver Fern. He wore a leather jacket that was too thin for the temperature and looked feverish.

"Oh sorry," I said as I jumped backwards out of the way, "I didn't see you."

"Not at all," he said, "my pleasure."

I tried to walk around the drunk, but when I moved to the left of him he moved left. When I tried again from the right to move around him, he moved that way too. The whole time he prevented me from sidestepping him, he had a sick grin pasted on his face like someone who was playing a very amusing game. After bumping into him several times, I noticed he had an awful smell even for someone who had spent the day in a bar. The man smelled like dried scabs and liquor and was a sickly shade of white. Knowing the staggering man was possibly about to get sick on top of me, made me want to avoid him even more. I tried to back away from him once more, only to have him grab at me.

Oh God help me! I had walked right into a pervert. Please don't touch me! What should I do?

I didn't want to turn my back on him, because then I would have to run deeper into the dead end street. But

Martin was in the house at the end of the block and if he knew a pervert was after me he would let me come in and call the police from inside the house.

I counted to three before running; one, two, three… and turned and raced towards the brick house at the end of the street. I wouldn't stop until I reached the door and pounded on it to be let in. I made it to the house in twenty seconds flat, but before I could put on the brakes, Martin and the girl appeared in the driveway.

They both had strange looks on their faces as if they expected me. Running as fast as I could, I careened right into the two of them to get away from the drunk and the girl harshly grabbed my arm.

Marney was smiling in triumph as she grabbed me by one arm, and reeled me in like a fish on a line. As for the vampire she was with- he only looked like Martin from a distance because he was young. The two of them had been using mind control on me so I would follow them from school.

In the past I had only seen glimpses of Marney. Kelly kept me and Marney separate from each other, and yet I recognized her immediately.

Marney had a complexion like boiled Cream of Wheat and large watery, red rimmed eyes. There was a hunger and loathing in her eyes, mixed with a certain desperation that only addicts have. The red lines running through her eyes betrayed the fact that she was addicted to a variety of substances. And her oversized dark pupils betrayed her thirst for blood.

The vampire standing next to her was a good likeness for Martin from half a block away. Up close, he was young and nice looking for a blood sucker and I could tell someone had made him a vampire while he was still a teenager. I expected Marney's friends to be old, decrepit horrible monsters, not so young or in this case attractive. The tall, greasy vampire was not so bad looking either when I realized he was after my blood and not something else more sinister.

My heart hurt, not from running, but from the dread of being surrounded by the three vampires. There was nowhere to hide and no way to outrun them, even if I managed to wrench my arm away from Marney.

The envelope Kelly had given me before she left, the one with the mysterious phone number scrawled on a piece of paper inside of it, was tucked behind me in my backpack. This was definitely an emergency, but unfortunately Marney wasn't going to let go of me for a minute so I could place a call to a vampire killer named Rex.

The two vampires with Marney would not stand still and were circling me like rabid dogs. There was no way to avoid my death; I prayed they were going to kill quickly me and not change me into a vampire. I didn't want to live out my years in servitude to Marney like

Kelly did. I did not want to be one of Marney's vampire protégés... death would be better.

"Where's Kelly?" Marney hissed when she got close enough to my neck to whisper into my ear. She ran her tongue up my carotid artery when she whispered and I winced.

"I don't know," I stuttered, "she left town when you bit her."

Marney's eyes flashed and she glared at me. "Liar, why would I bite Kelly, did she tell you that I bit her?"

Marney was appalled, as if I said something so distasteful, she couldn't believe I had dared to say it out loud. "Don't you know it's against the rules for vampires to bite other vampires?"

"Paul," said Marney to the greasy vampire, "would I bite Kelly?" Paul was extremely distracted either by being outside; he appeared to not get out much or by the proximity of all the delicious blood that flowed in my veins inches away from him. I would be a much appreciated hangover cure to him. He wouldn't mind tasting unadulterated blood for once.

Marney posed it another way, "did I bite Kelly, Paul?"

Paul was confused, like talking was foreign to him, especially when he would rather use his lips for drinking my blood.

"Answer me Paul!"

"No, Marney didn't bite her," Paul said licking his lips.

Paul was so close to me that he could grab me and end my life, and it caused a huge dilemma in waiting for him. It wasn't hard to read what Paul's mind... he couldn't help wanting my blood, any more then I could help wanting to breathe air and live.

"Walk with me Sinead," commanded Marney.

Obediently I fell into step with Marney and her companions. I was flanked by three vampires now. Paul behind me, and Marney and the teenage vampire I had mistaken for Martin on either side of me. I was sweating horribly as I walked between the three of them. The smell of my sweat was making Paul giddy; as he nudged me forward and sniffed the air as if he was trying to taste the air like a reptile would.

They were walking me towards the train tracks at the far end of the street. Even the boldest of vampires couldn't just kill their prey on an open street in broad daylight or what was left of it. People might catch them in the act and come after them, and if not people, vampire hunters, or other vampires. Vampires didn't like attention, so Marney had to be discreet, whatever she had in store for me.

When we got to the end of the sidewalk the youngest vampire grabbed my free arm and led me into the grass near the train tracks. We walked for another two hundred feet though the uncut grass, until we arrived behind a working factory. The second shift workers had been on duty for at least an hour or more, and there was a loud, vague sound of machines clacking away to meet production quotas. No one inside would hear me screaming over the machines. That was if I had time to scream.

Maybe if Marney left me when they were done, the workers would find my broken and drained body behind the building and notify the police. But what good would that do me if I was dead? And what could the police do to vampires? Anyway- Marney and her friends would be long gone to South America, leaving behind an unsolved mystery for my miserable parents.

"Now Sinead, where is Kelly?" asked Marney as she shoved me against the bricks of the factory.

"I don't know where Kelly is- she left to go hunting," I said.

"Kelly wouldn't leave you alone to fend for yourself; she was way too fond of you...,"

That made me smile, despite my desperate situation.

"You have two choices," Marney continued, "you can tell me where Kelly is and I won't kill you, but if you don't tell me where she is, I will let Paul kill you."

"If I tell you where Kelly is- are you going to let me go?" I asked.

"Perhaps I may let you go," said Marney, "but what I actually said is *if* you tell me where Kelly is, I won't kill you."

What Marney proposed didn't sound like much of a deal, but there wasn't any point to stalling, because I didn't have a plan. Maybe when they went to kill me, I could scream bloody murder banshee style. But turning into a banshee wouldn't faze these vampires at all. I would be a single firework going off before breaking bread. And it wouldn't do any good anyway because I would already be well on my way to becoming a vampire once Paul or Marney's teeth broke my skin.

"Hey," whispered the youngest vampire, "someone is coming out of the building."

"It's probably someone coming out on break. I needn't remind you to be quiet," Marney said to me as she delicately picked up my elbow and gave it a hurtful twist. I clamped my mouth shut and she twisted my arm a little more for good measure.

"Good girl," Marney whispered.

The back door to the factory opened and light spilled out on the parking lot. A worker came out of the door and looked around before lighting a cigarette. That gave me at least five or ten minutes to think. Maybe he would have two cigarettes and I could come up with something while he smoked. I wracked my brains trying to come up with a solution to the vampires surrounding me. I had nothing.

There wasn't anything to do but silently wait until the man finished his cigarette and went back in, so we waited. The man leaned against the bricks of the building and puffed on his cigarette a few times before stubbing it out on the asphalt and going back inside. The door closed shut again and the light retreated back into the busy factory. For some reason I craved a cigarette, even though I had never smoked.

With the man gone, Marney turned back to me and opened my coat away from my neck. Then she let go of my elbow and handed Paul my right wrist. The other vampire had already pushed the cuff of my coat up off of my left wrist.

My stomach did a somersault- the three of them were going to suck my blood simultaneously from three different directions. Even before the hungry vampires got started I felt the blood draining from my heart and I felt faint.

Paul's lips were on my wrist first, but before he broke my skin he looked toward heaven as if he was offering a prayer. Stunned by the notion of a praying vampire- I felt two long cool teeth glance off my wrist before Paul fell to his knees.

Paul was dead- pinned to the ground by a jagged stake! I looked down in shock at what was left of the vampire named Paul. A mess of blood pooled up from the wound in his chest and as the blood met the air, it hissed and burned.

The young vampire had already dropped my other wrist and fled- but it was too late. He too had been pinned by a stake made of a thick, heavy wood that had been sharpened into a deadly point. I didn't know where to look to avoid the gore, but when I looked down at my feet I saw that Paul's body had already disintegrated. All that was left was a charred, greasy stain in the dirt. I looked at the young vampire that had been staked against the factory wall and he was gone too. A smoldering stain was all that remained of him.

A blur streaked down the street and I caught a glimpse of the vampire hunter giving chase. Marney's ginger hair flashed as she ran out of the dead end street. I prayed the hunter would get her, but Marney disappeared. I wasn't sure what happened because she was too fast.

Grabbing my backpack that I had dropped earlier- I ran towards to the factory parking lot. A few more workers had come out for a smoke break and I was relieved to be in the company of people. My house was a few more blocks away and once I got home I would be safe. Turning the corner of the building, I ran straight into the man who had been smoking outside earlier.

"I came back to see if you were alright," he said.

"Why, who are you?"

"Nobody important," he smirked.

"Did you just kill those vampires?" I stammered.

He didn't answer me, but his eyes said everything. He was the man that came out for a smoke break. And after taking a few puffs of his cigarette he must have climbed to the top of the building. Leaping down unannounced, he staked Paul and Marney's young friend almost simultaneously. If he had three arms, Marney would have been dead too.

"Thank you for saving my life; I don't know how you were there at the right time."

"Thank Kelly. She sent me ..." he said in a gruff voice.

"How did Kelly know to send a vampire hunter at the right time?"

"Vampire hunter," the strange man laughed, "I'm no vampire hunter." The man offered me a wide grin before he disappeared into thin air.

My heart felt like it was going to explode against my rib cage after running home at a record pace. The back door slammed shut and I leaned into it to catch my breath. I was exhausted and frightened beyond belief, but safe in my own house. I used the last bit of energy I could summon to crawl up the stairs and into my bed. I was going to lay there and breathe deeply for as long as it would take to calm my nerves and get my frantic thoughts back in order...

Dark dreams haunted me that night. My body recovered quickly from running home but my mind was slow to coming around too. My mind was in shock and my subconscious was desperately trying to process everything that happened and then dispose of it. I didn't want to relive what had happened, but I couldn't forget the three vampires surrounding me. My bare skin itched where I had been touched by fangs. One thing I knew for sure- was that there were no vampires remaining in the area.

That morning I woke up relieved to be alive, but also feeling lonely. Kelly was not coming back for Christmas. She took a great personal risk to keep me safe from Marney and I was grateful about how things had turned out.

But the one thing I could not understand was why the vampire Kelly sent to rescue me killed the other vampires... It didn't make sense; vampires did not kill other vampires.

CHAPTER 8

Martin knew I was depressed about Kelly leaving but he wouldn't directly ask me about it. The two of us sort of had an unspoken agreement that we wouldn't talk about her, because it caused hard feelings. I wasn't sure what his reasons were, but he disliked Kelly intensely. I guess if I could put my finger on it- maybe at some deep instinctual level Martin knew that Kelly was dangerous.

Inside every animal, including the human animal- is the ability to read between the lines and to know who is being hunted and who the hunter is. This may be elementary stuff when you see a grizzly bear while hiking through a blueberry patch. But the line becomes blurry when the hunter looks *almost* exactly like what he is hunting. Not only that, but vampires could turn the tables on us, by making people want to get near them. So while most people were oblivious to Kelly's vampire nature and even attracted to her, I think Martin suspected that Kelly was a threat. And maybe that's why he couldn't see any redeeming qualities in her.

"Do you want to talk about anything?" Martin asked after school. It was the day before Winter Break.

I sighed because he didn't say *do you want to talk about Kelly…* It was just like him to want to talk, but not about her.

"Look, I can take a hint- I'll leave you alone," he said as he walked away.

Sometimes when we're locked in stubbornness, the natural world intervenes and pushes us back in the right direction. As if on cue, the steel gray winter sky opened up and a billion soft, white crystalline flakes swirled down creating a magical canvas. It was as if I was caught in a giant snow globe and there was nothing left for me to do but soften and melt.

I didn't want to be angry anymore.

Martin was still up ahead, but walking steadily away from me with his head bent towards the ground. More snowflakes fell, obscuring him and threatening to swallow him up.

I ran after him.

"Wait" I said as I reached out to intertwine my arm into the crook of his.

He did better than reaching for my arm and turned around, kissing me for the first time. Giant flakes melted on our faces. I looked up into his eyes and knew I wanted to be with him.

The room was unbearably hot, because I was seated too close to the fire. The hot chocolate scalded my tongue and the cookies crumbled, sweet and gritty on my burnt tongue. The Christmas lights blinked on and off so fast I felt seasick. I was uncomfortable enough and on top of everything, my Christmas sweater was itchy. From the corner of the room, Martin watched me, brooding. It was obvious to him that I was unhappy as usual.

Alice darted in and out from the kitchen with small plates of cookies and sweets, trying to appease us.

"I'll leave you two alone," Alice said as she left for the final time.

Martin plopped down next to me, popping a piece of fudge into his mouth, "Do you like me?"

"Of course, I do. Why would you even ask that?"

"You aren't happy to be here. It's Christmas Eve and you act like you are a million miles away."

"I don't want to talk about it. Let's try to have a nice time. Do you want to watch a movie?"

"No. What don't you want to talk about? You're talking about Kelly right? Why shouldn't we talk about her? You've been moping around ever since she left. There's something going on there and you never want to talk about it. I don't want to avoid this anymore... Is there something I should know?"

"No. I miss her and I don't want to talk about it with you, because I know you hate her and that makes it hard."

"I don't hate her- it's that..." he trailed off.

"It's what?"

"I can't explain it. But I think there's something wrong with Kelly or something bad about her- that I can't explain. Look I am sorry, that sounds stupid. There's nothing wrong with your friend. I get a bad feeling about her and I don't want you to be mad at me. Forget I even said anything."

"It's okay- I understand what you are trying to say."

"You do?"

He was surprised, but I knew exactly what he was talking about. How could I be mad at him because he guessed that Kelly was dangerous and unnatural? Unfortunately, I couldn't clear up the issue between us by telling him Kelly was a vampire even if he was my boyfriend.

"Yes- I understand. Kelly gives off strange vibes to a lot of people. But she was my first real friend. Before her, I was kind of a loner. She means a lot to me mainly because of that."

"So, why did she move?"

"She had to go away... Her family life is complicated, Martin."

"Do you guys still talk to each other?"

His question made me want to cry. Most friends still talk, or at least email from time to time after they move away from each other.

"No. We don't. Anyway- it's Christmas Eve- I don't want to talk about Kelly. I'm here with you and I don't want to talk at all."

I moved away from the fire and parked myself on the empty loveseat. Martin turned on the TV, the last half of *It's a Wonderful Life* was on.

Right after midnight, Martin walked me home. The sky was softly lit with the winter constellations and church bells were ringing to welcome Christmas morning. Before I went inside, Martin handed me a small wrapped package.

"Do you want me to open it now?" I asked.

"No, but I won't see you tomorrow. I have to go to my grandma's house. Open it in the morning and think about me."

"Okay," I said blushing in the dark.

Martin kissed me again before saying goodbye. I stood there, the small package heavy in my hand, as he walked home. He waved back at me once before closing his front door.

Before I got out of bed Christmas morning, I pulled the small package out from under my pillow and opened it. Inside the small box was a pendant with two entwined hearts on a chain. Martin hadn't said 'I love you' yet- was the necklace his way of saying it? I wanted to call him on the phone and ask, but I didn't want to break the spell.

I went downstairs, still dressed in my pajamas, with the necklace clasped at my throat. My mom was still in bed but I didn't mind waiting for her. She was depressed because my dad was traveling over the holidays and wouldn't be home this year.

My mom padded softly behind me into the kitchen and said, "Merry Christmas sweetheart."

"Hi Mom- Merry Christmas."

I was uncomfortable when she saw my new necklace. I wanted to tuck the pendant into my shirt, but it was too late.

"A gift from Martin?" she asked.

"Yes."

"It's lovely."

Thankfully, she didn't ask me any uncomfortable questions about Martin. Instead she made breakfast, while I went into the living room and shook some of the presents stashed under the tree. I was too old- I suppose to get up at the crack of dawn to open gifts or maybe Christmas wasn't exciting anymore.

There weren't tons of gifts under the tree, because it was just the two of us that Christmas. My dad was out of town on business for another month. And most of what was under the tree he had sent to us in the last week, things he had ordered online and had shipped to us. There were also a few packages from grandparents, aunts and uncles, and a fruitcake from a neighbor who enjoyed eating fruitcake.

Over the sounds of frying bacon and eggs, I heard my mom talking to someone in a soft voice. She was on the phone telling my dad how much she missed him and that we would love his presents. When it was my turn to talk- I told my dad I loved him and missed him too.

After saying goodbye I got off the phone and made short work of breakfast and then tackled the small stack of gifts under the tree.

When we were done opening gifts, my mom went into the kitchen to clean up the breakfast dishes and work on Christmas dinner. While she stayed busy in the kitchen, I cleaned up the wrapping paper and made small neat piles of her gifts and mine. Then I took her things to her bedroom and put them on her bed. The jewelry she received from my dad I put on top of her dresser, next to a small gift wrapped package.

"Hey, Mom did you forget a present?"

"I don't think so."

"What about this one?" I handed her the small package; it didn't have a name tag on it.

"Oh, that's right. A man delivered that yesterday afternoon. He said it was for you."

"For me- do you know who it's from?"

"Well- I thought it came from Martin. The man who dropped it off wasn't a delivery man; he looked like someone from around the neighborhood. I thought he might be Martin's uncle or a visiting relative. Anyway- he was odd. He was friendly but he gave me the creeps."

"And he said this was for me. Should I open it?"

"Why not, it can't bite you whatever it is. I thought it was from across the street… but it looks like you already got a present from Martin."

"That is weird."

"Well- open it. I am dying of suspense now," said my mom.

The paper tore away neatly and I opened the little foiled box. Inside it was a very old ring, an emerald ring if I wasn't mistaken. I recognized it right away- because it was a ring that Kelly wore.

"Wow- that looks real," said my mom peering into the box. "It's not an engagement ring is it?"

I knew what she was thinking. "Ummm- I think it is real, but no, it's not an engagement ring. It's from Kelly."

"I don't know if you should keep that ring," my mom said after she picked it and examined it. "It looks like an old family heirloom."

"It's alright, Mom, I will give it back to her. Don't worry about it. She probably didn't know what to get me and sent it along so I wouldn't think she forgot about getting me a present. It's a last minute present." The ring was a strange omen, but I didn't want my mom worrying about it.

"Oh- well that makes sense- I guess. By the way, where is Kelly, I haven't seen her in a long time?"

"She's out of town."

My mom gave me a puzzled look, she hated when I was vague about Kelly. But this time I really didn't have any answers for her.

Upstairs I tried on the ring. The deep green gemstone reminded me of Kelly's eyes and it was the first glimmer of hope I had in a long time. I took it as a sign that Kelly wanted me to remember her at Christmas. It was thoughtful, even if it would make everyone around me uncomfortable.

Pulling it off, I stashed the ring in the top drawer of my desk, so no one else could get upset by it. I couldn't wear the ring. Martin would be curious about where it came from and he might get mad if he found out it was from Kelly.

The ring wasn't a mystery to me; I knew what Kelly was trying to tell me. I was more curious about the man who delivered the gift, then the actual gift. Was the creepy delivery man my vampire rescuer from the factory? It was too bad I missed him when he delivered it to my house.

Martin was gone for a week. When he said he was going to his grandma's house, I thought he meant for the day. He was actually gone until New Year's Eve. With him gone so long and the meaningful gift he gave me, he had anticipation working overtime in his favor. I missed him so much; that I almost stopped thinking about Kelly the whole week of Christmas Break.

When Martin returned on New Year's Eve, he met me at my house.

"Did you like my present?"

"I love it," I said.

He didn't say anything. He didn't get the hint…"Did you mean it?" I asked.

"Mean what?" He smiled at me like he still had no idea what I was talking about.

"You know?"

"Hmm- I am not sure what you are talking about?"

"Does the necklace mean what I think it means?"

"What does the necklace mean?"

"I love you," I said.

"I love you too," he said and laughed.

"You got me to say it first!"

"And why not," he laughed some more, "it took me almost two months to find out if you even liked me, when I knew the minute I first saw you."

"Really?"

"Yes."

"What about Melanie Walker?"

"Who?"

"Oh give me a break."

"No really- that was nothing. She invited me to a Halloween party and I went with her to meet people. I didn't go to the party to be with Melanie, she's not my type…"

"Hmmmph!"

"Really- I love you."

He couldn't say it again, because I kissed him that time.

Looking back at the holidays, we were happy. There was no reason not to be; especially when you first fall in love… but what goes up must go down. January came and went; and we were still falling in love with each other. I can say that now without a doubt, but there was also something missing from our relationship. Sure I was sometimes distracted and moody because I still hadn't heard from Kelly, but there was tension underneath the surface between Martin and I that I could not fully understand then.

Our love wasn't as perfect as it appeared on the surface- it had a beautiful, fragile quality like a vase of cut flowers. It was beautiful to look at in the present moment, but in the back of my mind I knew our relationship wouldn't live on much longer.

We were happy and we rarely fought, but we also alternated between hot and cold with each other for no apparent reason. Sometimes it was Martin who was distant for reasons that had to do with his swimming competitively at school. During swimming, I wouldn't see him for days outside of school and so talking for twenty minutes at lunch was all we had to keep our relationship going on. Some days, I waited for Martin to walk home with me, only to find out he had already left for another practice swim, even though the swim team had the day off. And a few times, I called his house and Alice answered the phone and told me he wasn't at home… even though I was sure he was.

True- Martin was the star of the high school swim team, and he was very busy in the winter months with practice and meets. But he never gave me the impression that he was obsessed with competition. For the most part I gave him a lot of space then even though it was killing me inside, because I knew that swimming season would have to end sometime.

His behavior wasn't too strange when you put it into perspective. Martin was dedicated to seriously training for a sport. But at the time, some things struck me as odd. For one, he wouldn't let me attend any of his swim meets and that hurt. I felt left out of his life and I couldn't understand it- since I was his girlfriend. It sucked having to find out how Martin did by reading the meet results when they were posted on the school sport bulletin boards.

When I asked him about attending a meet, Martin gave me an excuse. He said that I was too much of a distraction for him. And I acted like this explanation satisfied me but it didn't. I felt hurt and excluded from something very important to him.

There was something odd about his mother during swimming season too. At first I was just jealous of her because Alice got to go to all his meets. But while she was proud of him, I felt like she didn't like Martin swimming either. She was in as much of a hurry as I was for swim season to be over. And at the time I actually thought she *hated* watching Martin swim. It was all an act- Alice being the proud swim team mother; because I knew Alice would be happy if Martin never stepped into a pool again.

February arrived without any change in the weather. The days were as cold as ever- the only difference was the days were slightly longer. Spring was still far away and I was anxious and unsettled inside.

As for Kelly, after all those weeks I resigned myself to the fact that she wasn't coming back anytime soon. The gift she left me, her ring, took on a new meaning for me. Instead of a promise that she would return- it became a souvenir of our friendship and a token of our long goodbye. And some days, I told myself that I didn't need her to come back since I had a boyfriend. I knew Martin wouldn't be happy if Kelly showed up in my life again.

But on my loneliest days I thought of Kelly often and tried to remember how it felt to let her in my head. It was during that dark winter that I discovered how hard it was to be lonely and how harder still it was to be lonely when you are a part of a couple. With Martin so wrapped up in swimming, it made me feel a little better to imagine that there was someone else in the world that still cared about me. It would be unbearable to think Kelly had forgotten me too. And so I reattached myself to that small hope- about a girl and her best friend...

Loneliness makes a girl do strange and needy things. One day after school, I surprised even myself by slipping into the girl's locker room side of the pool. It was quiet and dark in the girl's changing area and from behind the cracked open door to the pool room- I listened as the coach ran the boys through drills. The coach whistled and shouted out directions to each boy swimming in their lanes and I stood there for some time waiting for courage and the right moment to slip into the pool room with them.

When I knew for sure Martin was still in the water and wouldn't be able to see while swimming, I crept behind the bleachers and hid. Boys were in the water swimming laps in almost every lane. But one swimmer stood out from the rest. He was in the outside lane and he swam faster and more effortlessly than all the others. This swimmer was more than a full length ahead of everyone else and he cut through the water at high speed, barely coming up to breathe. The fastest swimmer wasn't much more than a sleek shadow barely making a wake in the water, but I knew it was my boyfriend.

Shocked, surprised- I am not sure how to describe my reaction when I saw Martin swimming for the first time. It was unreal the way he moved so naturally in the water and at the same time almost impossible that a human could swim like he did. Martin moved in the water as if the water was his only natural element.

Finally, seeing Martin swim for the first time, I could appreciate some of the dedication and discipline he had. And I could understand why he kept me away from his meets; maybe I was a distraction I conceded.

Some of the boys were leaving the water, done with their workout. I only planned on watching for a minute before quietly heading back into the locker room, but I was captivated by Martin swimming. And since some of the boys had already left the water, I wasn't sure how I could sneak back to the girl's locker room without getting caught.

Martin stopped at the edge of the pool and the coach was bent down over him giving him instructions. One of the boys spotted me. It was too late, someone yelled across the cavernous pool room, "HEYYYY-Martin your girlfriend is here."

Martin swung his head in my direction and there was a flash of anger on his face. Then his face softened and he waved at me before pulling himself out of the pool.

I was embarrassed. He was more than ninety-five percent naked and that's when I *really* noticed all the other boys in Speedos too. Someone handed Martin a towel, and he dried himself off while coming over.

"What are you doing in here?"

"Watching you swim. I'm sorry, but I heard how good you are and I wanted to see for myself. You won't let me go to your meets and they don't post videos around here unless it's a basketball game."

"Okay- I'm sorry I keep pushing you away. The season is almost over and I will have more time for us then. I promise. Look- I'm going to swim a few more laps, so you should probably go home. Things will be different soon, you'll see, in a few weeks."

I watched Martin slide back into the water before leaving. I was glad he didn't try to kiss me. He was so naked and wet; I didn't want to think about it. But I did feel somewhat better after I saw him swimming- at least he had a good reason for ignoring me.

ACT II - AN INTERLUDE

There aren't many rules to being a vampire, but there is one rule that is paramount. That rule being; a vampire is never to drink from another vampire. It's not something one does. And in my nightmares I often relive that day, when Marney turned on me in a drunken haze and drank my blood.

What I do remember clearly of that day- was that Marney was angry with me again. An addict is angry many times in a single day for no apparently good reason other than being irritated about being alive. What little infraction I may have made that day was not obvious to me and I strongly doubt if Marney could recall what I had done either to be treated that way.

Regardless the reason, Marney turned on me in a fit of rage and tried to drain all the blood in me. She would have succeeded too- if Gregory hadn't pulled her off of me. I still remember the look of horror on his face when he saw what Marney was doing.

After Gregory pulled Marney off of me, I managed to drag myself to the window and escape. When the cold air hit me in the lungs- it felt like a fire was ignited inside me and I fell to the ground in shock and disbelief. If Gregory hadn't shown up when he had, Marney would have drained me until I was completely empty, leaving me sprawled there on the carpet of my bedroom flopping around like a fish stranded without water.

And that is exactly what it feels like to have someone draw the blood out of you when you are a vampire. It is a pain so deep that I could only liken it to violently pulling the oxygen out of mortal lungs.

First, there is a medieval tearing and sucking sensation as the blood is pulled and stripped from your arteries and veins, leaving one with an intense sensation of being empty and raw. Next, there is an excruciating burning that occurs when the arteries and veins are depleted of blood and they start to dry up and shrivel shut.

True this wouldn't have killed me, because there are few things that can kill a vampire; staking, being one of them. Perhaps being shot in the heart with silver or burned in fire, but those methods are old ones that I am not familiar with. In reality- I have only known vampires that were killed by being staked through the heart. So although Marney draining me would not have killed me, it was a pain I would never wish to relive even if I live to be a million years old.

Not only was there an acute physical pain, but a psychological wound was inflicted as well. Not by Marney alone I might add, some of this wound was of my own making… as I should have left Marney at least twenty years ago and yet I allowed myself to stay in a subservient, embarrassing position for so long.

And that's where I came back into this story with this burning ember of bitterness lodged in my chest that burned every time I breathed.

The only thing in the last few years that saved me from being absolutely miserable was Sinead. For almost a century, I had probed the minds of others looking for someone sympathetic to my condition. I still remember the first day I read Sinead's mind. Barely perceptible then, there was something entirely foreign and almost animal in her brain that I could not clearly read or understand.

She was a mystery to me. At the time I didn't know that the primal thing I had touched on in her brain was her reaction to death. It wasn't until later when I saw her react on Halloween night near Calvary cemetery that I knew without a doubt that there was a strange and beautiful kindred spirit in her. And so our friendship means a lot to me, as Sinead also struggles with finding purpose and meaning in being an unnatural creature in this world.

As excited as I was about meeting her, Sinead was initially repulsed by me as most people are who are not actively being manipulated by a vampire. It is only by guile and manipulation that humans are attracted to vampires like bees attracted to pollen. So I was very careful to not manipulate or coerce her in any way that could be construed as giving me an upper hand in our relationship. From the outset, I wanted our friendship to be natural and mutual. And without this coating of guile and predatory manipulation Sinead resisted me and naturally didn't want anything to do with me. It took sometime after our first meeting to win her trust and to me it was as short of time as any for someone who may have centuries before them.

As you can imagine, it was difficult to leave Sinead alone with Marney, Paul and Gregory still living near her, but it was finally time for me to extricate myself from Marney.

After I left Sinead, I traveled to Phoenix not to prey on homeless people but to be seen by other vampires. I wanted to carefully distance myself from what would occur in Wisconsin during my absence. And the only foolproof way to make sure I was not implicated in what was to become of Marney was for others of my kind to see me elsewhere.

When I left Sheboygan- I didn't leave Sinead entirely alone. There was a fifth vampire residing in our area, I was well acquainted with. His name was Rex and we had both been vampires for relatively the same amount of time. Give or take a few years, he was human born in 1892 and made a vampire in the year 1919. Ironically, Rex and I met in the 1940s during the war through mutual friends of Marney. We were both idealistic then and still feeling our humanity at the time. Back then Rex was a kinder and gentler soul, as far as vampires went. He was one of those odd vampire types that believed there was a difference in innocents and evil people, whether they were human or otherwise. And after losing touch with each other for approximately sixty years, I was surprised to find out Rex was staying in almost the same area as I was when Marney brought her little band of vampires to live on the bluff in Sheboygan.

After locating Rex, it took very little effort to convince him to keep an eye out on Sinead. From living and hunting in the same area, Rex already knew what Marney, Paul and Gregory were about. To say he was less than impressed with them was an understatement.

To be honest, I wasn't surprised when I had heard that Rex put a stake through Paul and Gregory... not in the least. I certainly didn't ask him to use extreme force on them to keep Sinead safe, but I wasn't surprised. Rex still had a soft spot for weak people, such as the young ravers that Marney and her friends lured into clubs with promises of free drugs.

As for Rex, he wouldn't prey on anyone who wasn't outright evil and couldn't put up a good fight. I imagine Rex was tired of their foolish games and addictions and would have put a stop them sooner or later even without me asking him to watch over Sinead. And watch over her he did, because when the time came he saved Sinead from a disastrous end. My only regret beyond leaving Sinead in the first place, is that Rex did not kill Marney too that night, because she was the only one of the three that was truly dangerous. And I was sort of sentimental towards Gregory.

After a month or so had passed from when Rex killed Paul and Gregory, I moved north again. The vampires in Phoenix were quite welcoming and fond of new company being a friendly, bohemian lot. But the truth was I had always been an outsider, having been changed by Marney as a teenager and still having a brain that alternated between juvenile and adult. And this always left me feeling like I was an anomaly in the vampire world. I had developed the speech and mannerism of an adult but in the end felt more comfortable around people my own biological age.

I did enjoy the variety of animal game in Arizona and the different scenery, but I was dying to get back to Wisconsin and finally reunited with Sinead. But since I still needed to put space and time between that gruesome incident, I moved slowly north, traveling in a circuitous northwestern direction until I found myself in Canada.

Canada was a unique diversion, as it was a wild and ruggedly beautiful hunting ground. But I was ill at ease there until I was back in the states. The brief time I spent in Canada I felt as though I was being closely watched and it was quite unsettling. Finally, in mid-February I stepped over the American border and traveled back down through Wisconsin to my previous home.

Of course the house that Marney and I had lived in with the others was no longer my home. There was no way I would return to live in a house filled with so many bad memories. Besides, the house had probably reverted back to the bank's ownership and would soon be filled by a new family, one not so devoid of humanity and reasonable behavior.

When I arrived back in Sheboygan, I found a nicely furnished, empty apartment over Eighth Street facing the coffee shop that Sinead and I used to frequent. And I settled into the apartment as soon as I knew it was unoccupied for a considerable time. I wasn't about to bother with manipulating the landlord for the key or paying for a rental.

Settled into my new home, I wasn't sure I was ready to see Sinead again. I still didn't feel like my old self. In the past I used to be optimistic and lighthearted or so I thought… but when I returned I was restless, agitated, and most of all angry with myself. It wasn't a good idea for me to reconnect with humans yet, let alone my best friend. I didn't want Sinead to see me like this either, in this doubtful spirit, questioning everything about myself and my moral character. Although part of me wanted to seek her out immediately, the other more reasonable part of me told me to wait. Without my rational mind working satisfactorily I was dangerous to Sinead and I never wanted to hurt her.

Sometimes I doubted Sinead was still expecting me to come back. Had she had moved on without me? And then I would remember how it felt to read the thoughts and emotions in her mind. Repulsion, anger, fear, happiness and wonder- they were all inside of her in glowing human tinted colors and wonderful to feel.

One of the few upsides to being a vampire is the inexplicable joy to be found in perusing someone's mind and their emotional states. Vampires have this small miracle of deep connection through the mind. It's exhilarating to subtly feel the raw emotions of another person. It is no small feat for a vampire to connect with another human being in this way. And what is even more remarkable was that I had connected with Sinead- who as a banshee had a distinctly supernatural and unusual outlook on the world.

The first few weeks I was back, I stayed around the downtown area near Lake Michigan. I slept through most days, only waking to spend evenings hunting for deer or small game in nearby Ozaukee County. When I wasn't feeding I walked about the small city trying to soothe my mind. Sometimes I read books from the library and when I felt as sociable as a vampire gets, I would go down to Paradigm and listen to bands play or the spoken word poets perform.

I wasn't sure how much longer I was going to avoid Sinead, maybe for a few more weeks or so until I got up the courage to see her again. But one night while I was walking downtown, I saw a figure that looked remarkably like Sinead walking towards me on the other side of the street. Her head was down against the wind and she wasn't alone. It wasn't difficult for me to make myself invisible to the two of them, and so I did, so I could observe them. It wasn't like Sinead to be out with other people, so I was surprised to see her in the company of a boy, and I found myself spying on her.

The couple- for they were clearly a couple and holding hands, walked into Paradigm and sat on a couch near the window. I recognized the boy, his name was Martin and he was with Melanie Walker on Halloween night when she had her unfortunate accident. Seeing Sinead and Martin together, made me feel like I was intruding. And yet I wanted to barge in and talk to her, even though it was clearly not the right time. I needed to talk to Sinead when she was on her own and when I was back to a more reasonable version of myself, so I left them alone with their privacy intact.

That night in my apartment, I had mixed feelings. I was happy for Sinead; she was obviously in a relationship. But something dark inside of me stirred that was not happy or rational; I felt left out of Sinead's life and saw her new relationship as a dark omen.

It was easy to undo the window lock to her bedroom from the outside and slip inside her room. It would be easy to wake her without startling her, but I would have to exert a little mind control over Sinead to insure she was absolutely quiet, and it was something I did with some regret.

Sinead stirred quietly as I moved her arms to gently wake her. I focused my mind on giving her peaceful thoughts as she woke up slowly. Her eyes still focused on fragments of dreams.

"Kelly- is that you?"

"Yes Sinead, are you glad to see me?"

"Of course," she said sitting up, "how long have you been back?"

"Not very long," this was true to some extent.

"Marney's gone now and her friends were killed."

"I know."

"They tried to kill me, but another vampire came out of nowhere and staked them. Marney got away though…" Sinead trailed off; she was still worried about Marney.

"Sinead- I am sorry I put you through all this and without me here to protect you. I hope you can forgive me, but I had to leave for several reasons."

There was nothing but kindness and understanding in her sleepy eyes. I hoped this was all her and not any form of manipulation on my part.

"It's okay- I understand. I'm safe. You're safe, everything worked out in the end. I was scared that night, terrified actually but I'm over it. I actually got over it quicker than I expected. You're rubbing off on me- I am less afraid of things then I used to be."

Apparently she had gotten over many things- including her shyness. I knew that from seeing her with her new boyfriend, but I didn't say anything about that. I was glad to hear that I had some good influence on her.

"I am going to leave now so you can go back to sleep. I just wanted you to know that I am back and nearby in case you need me. Even if you don't see much of me- I am around," I said.

"Why won't you be around?"

"It's complicated, but everything will be fine. I need to keep some distance between me and what happened to Paul and Gregory." The part about Paul and Gregory was partially true, but there were other more important reasons that I kept hidden from her.

"Are those the vampires that got killed?"

"Yes."

"Okay- I think I understand. Kelly?"

"What is it?"

"Did you know the vampire that killed Paul and Gregory?"

"Yes, he and I are well acquainted."

"Will you tell me about him?"

"At a later time, I will tell you everything you want to know about Rex. But right now I need to leave and he isn't important."

"His name is Rex? I knew that, you left me his phone number."

Actually I didn't leave his phone number for Sinead to physically call on her cell phone. It was enough for Sinead to think about calling Rex at the time of trouble. In the future I would explain to Sinead how powerful a vampire's mind could be.

"Yes- I did. I have to leave now." Sinead's mother was stirring downstairs. She was on alert ever since her husband had left on business. If we kept talking, we would wake her unless I used manipulation on her as well and my prohibition on using mind control on Sinead was extended to her family too.

"Goodnight Sinead- I'll be back soon."

"Goodnight Kelly, I'm glad your back," Sinead said as she tucked herself back under her blankets.

"So am I."

I quietly went out the same way I came in and locked her window from the outside. When I looked back from the ledge, Sinead was already asleep again. I wasn't sure what I expected to accomplish that night. But for what it's worth, my spirits were raised and I was less dark and moody at least temporarily.

After that night, I stayed away from Sinead for several more weeks. I still didn't want to call any unwanted attention towards her and I. Rex had left the area as well and the deaths of Peter and Gregory would soon be ancient news.

There was a large coven residing in the luxury apartments on Lake Shore Drive in Chicago that were quite influential in the vampire world. I was being honest when I vaguely alluded to them taking interest in the deaths of Peter and Gregory. I didn't know how they would react to what had transpired. If we were lucky the Lake Shore Drive coven wouldn't be interested at all or even lift an eyebrow in our direction. Rex wasn't concerned, nor were the vampires I met in Phoenix. But I was concerned about Sinead and I left her alone in case being around her brought her to the attention of someone from my world.

If I am being totally honest though, there was a darker reason that I stayed away from Sinead. After being bitten by Marney I did the unthinkable. The same night I left Sinead after I fled Marney- I drank human blood and not once but twice...

I would like to say it was the extreme thirst after being almost completely drained by Marney that made me do it. And weeks later in Phoenix I even rationalized that there were drugs in my system from being bitten by that god-forsaken creature! But whatever excuses I made and blame I tried to place on someone else did not change the fact that I took two people's lives. Yes, I took the lives of the two humans I drank from.

I didn't want to speculate as to what Sinead would think of me if she knew that I had murdered innocent people, let alone drank their blood as if they were common cattle. At the time, I believed it would end our friendship, because it would be a complete breach of all the fragile trust she had in me.

As for trust on the part of Sinead, I have to say I hardly trusted myself anymore in the company of humans. And sadly I had to admit that I couldn't be trusted around Sinead at least for the near future. Not only had I drank human blood again, but I was craving it nightly despite all my objections to the poor quality of the human diet and a lack of purity in their blood.

It was as if abstaining for so long and then partaking of that dark delight had opened a thirst that could not be quenched without a whole fount of human blood being spilt. And this thought terrified and excited me all at once. I was truly miserable about becoming a monster and tried to be penitent by punishing myself and staying away from Sinead. And I believed that if I had left Marney earlier with my dignity intact I would have never gone down this dark, evil road that I now traveled.

So many things had recently gone wrong in my life… I stayed with Marney in a toxic, subservient role for so long that it eroded my true nature. It was I who allowed myself to be abused and shamed. And when I finally fled the situation, in a fit of madness I killed two innocent lives to assuage my awful thirst. To heap more insult on injury, I left my only friend defenseless to face Marney, Paul and Gregory- possibly alone. Yes, I did enlist the help of Rex to keep watch over her, but in the end that decision cost two more lives as well. And although I could never wish anything less than the death of Marney; Paul and Gregory were just cogs in the machine and unintentional victims.

I can't believe the risk I put Sinead at with those three. Rex is a competent vampire, but still he was outnumbered and one can never be too careful when it comes to a human life. Sadly- I learned this lesson painfully on my own and only too well.

It was better at this point if Sinead thought that I was lying low as if I were afraid of some divine retribution from the vampires living in Chicago, than to know the truth that I was again a murdering, blood thirsty creature of the night. To put her through that much fear and risk only to have her find out she was at a later risk of death by me- would be too much to put on her and our relationship.

It would break us.

CHAPTER 9

There was a dark figure in my bedroom. Someone stood in the shadows watching me while I slept. First they appeared in the landscape of my dream, walking towards me and next slowly moved my arms and shoulders rousting me out of the troubling dream. My response was fear and repulsion- but then the frightening apparition spoke comforting words inside my head. The voice was familiar.

"Wake up Sinead, its Kelly... I'm here and everything is fine. Wake up."

When I heard her voice, I knew it wasn't a dream. Kelly was back. And under the cover of darkness we talked for a short while. And when she left I fell back into a dreamless sleep.

Rested- but confused in the morning, I couldn't remember most of our conversation. I did know she was back and staying nearby, but that I still wouldn't see her for quite some time.

It had to do with the killings. I think Kelly was afraid that other vampires would find out that she sent Rex to kill Marney and her friends. Maybe that was it and Kelly was still hiding to protect herself from being attacked.

After her nighttime visit- I was relieved to see her again. But after a few more weeks passed without hearing anything more from Kelly, I began to doubt that she actually appeared in my bedroom that night. It was all a dream.

The mind plays strange tricks on people when they are separated. It's funny how you can be so sure of a person when they are always around and you have plenty of face time. But later when you are separated; you can have such horrible suspicions about them. And not only suspicions about them, but suddenly doubt everything you once knew was true about them and about your relationship. They say *absence makes the heart grow fonder*, but absence can also cast a long shadow of doubt on everything. And once the shadow falls, the lines between love and hate blur into strange and unusual configurations.

I loved Kelly- and for a time she was my dearest and only friend. But because she was also a predator there was this natural repulsion on my part and the longer she was gone, the more I was unsure about us. I was getting angry and disappointed the longer we stayed separated. We had a lot of fun together and I expected it to go on indefinitely into the future and instead she left me alone and vulnerable. I hated that she left me, and I despised her for leaving me hanging.

And this didn't make me feel good.

So instead of hating Kelly for leaving- I put up a wall of indifference towards our separation. But it hardly worked.

At the same time, there was an unhappy push and pull in my relationship with Martin as well. True, I had very little idea of how romances were supposed to work outside of books. But I did know that what we had was not a fairy tale romance.

During swimming season Martin was a whole different person, and he wasn't interested in our relationship. Looking back on it- he was going through the motions and maintaining our relationship by doing the very minimal work that would keep us going until after swim season ended.

So after the season ended, I expected things to get better and that Martin would have more time for me. I knew he would still have other outside interests besides me, but I didn't know that I would continue to be a very small part of Martin's life.

The rare times we shared together were wonderful, but Martin could be very distant and it bothered me. He told me he loved me, but it was hard to believe when he could be so uncaring and cold at times.

Wasn't love supposed to feel different?

We definitely were not madly in love with each other.

"I want to go to a hotel this weekend," Martin said after kissing me slowly.

"Uh- wow, uh I am not sure I am ready for that."

Martin winked at me and pulled me closer. "Not that silly, my cousin works at The Road Inn, they have a pool."

My happy little mood instantly plummeted; I thought we were past swimming season…

"Hey, don't frown- I'm not going to make you watch me practice. The season is over. What else is there to do in the winter- movies, bowling, eating? Do you want to go out to eat all the time? Swimming is a lot better than bowling…"

It actually did sound kind of fun. But what would my mom say about going to a hotel with Martin; I guess I would cross that bridge when I got there.

Fortunately for me- Alice must have smoothed it over with my mom. Sometime before the weekend- my mom went over to Martin's house to introduce herself to Alice. It was probably more likely that my mom wanted to know the deal about Martin and I going to a hotel, but that's a mom for you. Over coffee and Alice's delicious cookies, Alice told my mom that Martin's older cousin worked at the hotel and had gotten approval for Martin to swim in the hotel pool on the weekends. Martin had been swimming there a lot actually, because it was good for him to be in the water, relaxing and not competing.

On the drive over to The Road Inn, my mom tried to make small talk. I could tell she was nervous and wanted to have one of those uncomfortable mother/daughter talks in the car. What she didn't know was that I wasn't interested in having sex; at least not yet. It's not that I didn't enjoy being with Martin and not that I didn't have those kind of feelings. But my life was complicated- with my best friend missing and with me being a banshee. I wasn't even sure how I stood with Martin. And even though Martin was fun to be with, I felt like we could break up at any moment if we weren't careful.

I wasn't about to give up my virginity to Martin, only to get dumped shortly after. Being abandoned by my best friend had the effect of making me very wary of being dumped again. I had a lot of trust issues then, that I didn't have before my friendship with Kelly. If you think you might have trust issues, wait until you get dumped by a vampire.

Martin was waiting for me in the lobby. He looked small and sweet sitting in a high back chair with his swim team bag on the floor between his feet. Martin got up to meet me and my mom when we entered the lobby. And then he introduced us to his cousin, George who was behind the front desk playing solitaire online. After introducing us to George, Martin showed my mom the dressing rooms and the pool area.

My mom tried to act casual as she peeked into the pool room from behind the glass doors, but there was relief in her eyes when she saw the separate changing rooms and the little kids playing Marco Polo in the pool.

After silently deeming everything wholesome enough for her standards she went to leave.

"Call me when you need a ride," she said finally.

"That's okay, Mrs. Smith, I can give Sinead a ride. I got my license a couple weeks ago," said Martin.

My mother's face fell slightly; she was trying to find the exact words she was looking for before speaking.

I smiled at her, and said, "I'll call you when I need you."

That seemed to appease my mom and she went to leave again. I elbowed Martin in the ribs, when she turned her back on us and disappeared out the front door.

"What? What did I say?" asked Martin.

In the dressing room I changed slowly and then checked myself out in the mirror a few times before wrapping a towel around my torso. I was dressed in a modest one piece swimsuit. I hoped Martin wasn't wearing his swim team Speedos that left nothing to the imagination.

Martin must have been in the men's changing room, because he wasn't in the pool area. I took a seat in one of the plastic chairs next to the pool to wait for him and watched the children playing in the water. The kids bounced and bobbed around with plastic blow up toys and were having a water fight in the shallow end.

Several minutes passed- what was keeping Martin? A dark shadow moved fast under the water in the deep end of the pool. It was a little frightening, like a shark in the pool, but since I wasn't in the water yet I wasn't alarmed. I had to be seeing things. I looked over at the kids in the pool again, but they were oblivious to the shadowy thing in the water and splashed anything that moved.

I got up and slowly walked to the deep end of the pool to get a closer look. The shadow disappeared. I was seeing things. I walked to the other side of the deep end but still nothing. The water was cloudy and dense at the bottom. And still, there was no movement in the water at all. I must have imagined it. A hand shot out of the water and grabbed my ankle.

I screamed!

But just a little. The kids in the pool stopped splashing for a few seconds to stare at me before bursting into laughter. Martin looked up at me grinning from ear to ear.

"Nervous? I won't bite."

"No, I'm not nervous; I didn't know you were in there," I gestured at the deep end of the pool.

"Who did you think it was- the bogeyman?"

I tried to laugh, but it sounded like I was choking on chlorine. "I thought you were still in the dressing room."

"No, I've been waiting for you- are you going to get in?"

"It looks cold."

"It is, but you get used to it and then it's really nice."

"Hmmm."

Martin squinted at me. "You can't swim right? Is that it?"

"I'll go hang out in the shallow end and watch you," I nodded at the children wearing blow rings and riding animal shaped floats.

"That wouldn't be much fun. I'm here. You'll be safe so just hop in and I'll have you swimming in no time."

Martin patted the pool ladder. Inhaling deeply, I threw my towel onto a plastic chair and eased myself down the aluminum ladder and into the deep. Martin must have seen the look of sheer terror on my face because he stopped horsing around and was all business; it was very sweet. When he found out that I couldn't swim at all, he didn't try to put the moves on me or try to scare me. Instead he ran me through some basic swimming moves, like floating, kicking, and later the American crawl.

After I put some work into learning to swim, we spent the rest of the time floating and maneuvering around the deep end. Most of the time, I clung to the side of the pool, watching Martin weaving through the water effortlessly.

The children who were in the shallow end had left a long time ago and the water was dark and peaceful as I floated in the safety of Martin's arms. For the first time in many months I was at peace. The water and his arms had the effect of calming and soothing me.

"Do you want to get out and get something to eat?" asked Martin.

"No, I don't want this moment to end. It's so peaceful here with you."

Martin pulled me close to him and kissed me. Electricity ran through my body like a current. Underneath the excitement in his kiss was a small undercurrent of fear. I was afraid and shivered.

"Are you alright?"

Someone was watching us, but the room was empty. The only person nearby was George behind the front desk. He bounced his head to a song playing on his computer and ignored us. Outside the large glass windows, snow was falling under the sodium colored lights and the parking lot was empty. Still- it felt like someone was outside the glass walls looking at us like two fish in a bowl. I shivered some more.

"I'm cold," I said. "I changed my mind, let's eat."

Pulling myself up the ladder, I grabbed my towel off the chair and ran to the dressing room. Inside I showered with both eyes wide open, listening for someone else in the cavernous room. I was alone- I hoped. I dried myself off and dressed quickly, so I wouldn't be alone for long.

Back in the lobby, Martin was already waiting for me with his cousin. Bent over the large desk, they were carefully pouring over a pizza menu from Spicoli's.

"Martin wants to order anchovies, but I told him not around a girl…"

"Hey- I like fish, don't you?" asked Martin.

"Not really, and definitely not on pizza- I'm with George can't we get sausage or pepperoni?"

"Pepperoni is boring," said Martin.

But it was too late; George was already on the phone ordering two large meat pizzas for us without anchovies.

CHAPTER 10

It was a mistake to spy on her… clearly the lines between keeping my eye on Sinead and stalking her had blurred. Initially I told myself, I was keeping an eye on Sinead for her own safety and perhaps I was in the beginning. But as things progressed, the darker animal in me won out and I was stalking my victim.

I can still say with all conviction that I never would have intentionally killed Sinead. But unfortunately every animal instinct in me was reawakened after that dark night I drank human blood again. And once I was back in Sheboygan- it wasn't exactly Sinead that set my animal instincts on fire - it was someone else.

It had taken some time, but the horrible thirst for human blood finally subsided somewhat after several months and I thought I could be around Sinead again. A steady diet of animal blood and desensitizing myself again to humans as much as possible was working. I felt like my old self again, ready to resume reentry into the human world, if not at high school, at the least with Sinead. That's when I started watching Sinead and visiting her at night. In the beginning, I only went to her while she was sleeping and it went well. And I took comfort in the fact that I could be with her and not have any thirst around her.

I didn't try to wake her or talk to her as I did when I first got back. I didn't want to manipulate her feelings toward me under the circumstances. At the time I felt that I was still capable of making sound decisions and that I was merely proving the point that she was safe with me again even at her most vulnerable; asleep in bed.

After several weeks of visiting Sinead at night, I watched her at school, wandering our high school unnoticed by the other students. It was nice to be back within the confines of my old school and around the people I was once attached to. As a predator I recognize people by smell and it was comforting to smell the familiar smells of my former school mates. But even more reassuring was the fact that I was not attracted to any of the students in that I wanted to make a meal out of any of them.

Curiosity led me to watching Sinead more and how she responded to her world without her knowing I was there. I was taking certain liberties with her privacy by spying on her, but in my mind I was still making sure she was safe from me…

When I watched Sinead, she was very unhappy. And I was interested to find out what was causing her so much sadness. Sinead was never comfortable in her skin, because she was different from the others- a banshee, but this was more than discomfort. Her sad mood had nothing to do with her unnatural abilities which were almost forgotten by her.

I hoped that it didn't have anything to do with me leaving, but I knew that I was probably to blame for the majority of her distress. Sinead was in a new relationship and I thought it would make her feel less slighted by me leaving her, but it didn't seem to help much.

At first, I kept my distance from her relationship with Martin, thinking it would be too much of a violation of her privacy for me to spy on them together. But seeing her unhappy day after day, made me cross over that boundary as well and I soon found myself watching them for clues to her unhappiness. I watched them eating lunch and walking home at night. And I watched them nesting on the couch huddled over coffees at the coffee shop that Sinead and I used to frequent. They were like any other couple in love. So why wasn't she happy with him?

There were little things that I noticed. For instance, in the beginning Martin wasn't very involved in the relationship and it appeared to have everything to do with being the captain of the swim team. During the winter sports season he had very little interest in anything outside of swimming and that included his relationship with Sinead. In retrospect, I guess he was a normal competitive sportsman, showing discipline and intense focus.

And then as soon as swimming season ended, Martin went from aloof and holding Sinead at arm's length to being more attentive. And that was the start of a blossoming love, which made me uncomfortable. At first I was jealous of Martin being with my friend. Sinead was no longer the isolated, introverted person that she was when I had initially met her and I felt threatened by her changing relationship with Martin.

In the early days of watching their relationship I felt an intense jealousy over Sinead… but then something changed and I was no longer jealous of losing her. The more I watched them together, the more things blurred and I was soon becoming jealous of *her* and jealous of her relationship with Martin. And I began to think she was treating him poorly, by being so miserable. Sinead should have been happy and grateful to be with Martin.

It was as if all the tension lines in me had suddenly snapped and my ability to be rational had broken down. I had crossed a line I should have run from. I can't pinpoint the moment it occurred, but somehow it did- I wanted to be with Martin. I wanted to be the one in his arms. I wanted to share a million kisses with him and feel his hot breath inside my mouth- warming me from the inside out. My attraction to him was sudden and irrational and soon I couldn't remember a time when I didn't feel this way. And not only did I want to be with him, but I wanted to make him mine forever. I wanted to drink deeply of the fountain of his blood. For the first time in my life, I wanted to make a vampire.

I would make Martin completely and thoroughly mine.

For a while there was still a shard of sanity left in me and I tried to keep my sinister desires and evil fantasy in check. I would remind myself that making a vampire was wrong and that this was a dark dream I had no business indulging in. And when my desire for Martin got too strong, I would flee across the border to hunt in Canada and feast on animal blood for many nights at a time. Sometimes before I returned I would feel sane again and even cured of my desire for human blood. Only to have it return as a debilitating addictive need when I was back home in Wisconsin and near Martin.

And soon I was no longer leaving on hunting trips and no longer clearing my mind of my devilish thoughts. In fact, I started feeding them and constructing horrible plots against Sinead *and* Martin. An anger that should have been directed at Marney or myself started to manifest against my dearest friend Sinead. She was a toxin in my life- another poisonous entity in my life that was holding me back from happiness.

If it was only a blind rage I would have killed her, luring her into the forest like Snow White. Drinking her down to the last drops as her life ebbed away. But this wasn't blind rage; it was a dark and calculating evil madness that had come over me. I wanted to keep her alive so she could see me take away the thing that mattered to her most.

The more I brooded on these dark thoughts, the stranger my perceptions became. I no longer saw Sinead as the vulnerable banshee girl who needed my help to maneuver her way in this world. She was no longer the naïve and innocent supernatural girl who stood beside me in a hostile world... I saw her as a strange siren, who had seduced Martin and held captive the one person who could make me happy.

I couldn't explain my attraction to Martin. Only that I desperately wanted him and that Sinead had him was enough for me to unleash the full brunt of my anger and bitterness on her. And so I devised a plan.

CHAPTER 11

In my three years of high school, I never expected to get excited about junior prom. Maybe it was no surprise to everyone else that Martin asked me to the prom, that was to be held at the end of April, but for me, it was nothing short of a miracle. For as long as I could remember, even back to middle school, I sat on the sidelines of every single school dance hoping that some boy would ask me to get up and join him on the dance floor.

So in the weeks leading up to junior prom, everything- including homework, family, and even Kelly took a back seat to all my fantasizing and planning for this dance. There was hair and nails to be done and an outfit to be coordinated and assembled. But the most important detail in my mind was the dress. I didn't want a shiny, tarty gown from off the formal rack. I wanted something different, maybe vintage and definitely romantic. And I spent long nights after school browsing vintage shops online for the perfect dress.

Finally- I found a beautiful vintage dress in my size that suited me perfectly, but it was more money than I had in my bank account at the time. Unconcerned about the cost, I knew I could easily save up the money and have it shipped before prom if I got down to making money right away.

In the meantime- I had shoes to pick, and accessories and makeup to find in order to match my perfect dress. And then one evening when I went to look online at the dress to color coordinate it with a pair of shoes- it was gone. I immediately emailed the seller to ask about it and she told me it had sold! I couldn't believe it- it had taken me several weeks to find the perfect vintage prom dress and in my size. I was so upset about this last minute disaster- I started to cry.

"What's wrong Sinead?" asked Alice.

I waited until Martin left the room to get his homework notes from his bedroom, before answering his mom.

"I wanted something different to wear at junior prom so I looked for a vintage dress online. Anyway, I found the perfect dress, but I didn't have enough money to buy it."

"How much is the dress?" Alice asked.

"It *was* three hundred dollars."

"How much money do you have, do you want to borrow some money from me?"

"No- that's not it. Thank you, though. I have the money now. The thing is, the dress sold a couple days ago while I was still earning enough money for it. And since it was vintage, there was only one in stock. Now it's almost prom and I can't find anything like it. I don't want to buy something off the rack."

"Oh. Do you have a picture of the dress? I'd like to see it."

"Yeah- I can show you a picture of it on my phone."

Alice looked at the dress. "It's pretty."

"You like it?"

"Yes- it reminds me a little of my wedding dress. The wedding dress styles when I got married were still these horrible puffy, awful things from the eighties even though it was the nineties. I didn't want to look like a puffed marshmallow, so I bought a prairie dress from a thrift store. It was a lovely dress."

"Do you have a picture of your wedding; I would love to see it?"

"I can do better than that- I can show you the dress. It's in the attic. Do you have time or is your English project waiting?"

Did I have the time? Asking me to look at a dress was like asking me if I wanted to eat or breathe.

"Yeah," I said, "let me tell Martin what I'm doing."

In the hallway, Alice pulled down a set of folding stairs from the ceiling and I followed her up them. Inside the attic, stacks of boxes lined the walls; it would be a fun place to explore if I was five years younger. Alice pulled a chain on a bare light bulb fixture, before rummaging through a pile of boxes in the farthest corner.

"I'm not sure why I kept this dress, but I really liked it," said Alice as she pulled out a wedding gown presentation box and handed it to me.

I peeked at the dress through the clear plastic front, not expecting much. It was a wedding dress and I was still mourning the loss of the perfect prom dress. Prom dress; wedding dress- these were obviously two different things.

Alice's wedding dress was not what I expected. It was covered in so many small pink flowers that the dress appeared pale pink not white. A wide pink ribbon ran under the high empire waist just under the breast and the dress had small capped short sleeves. It was more Regency style, then prairie. A few strains of a waltz sounded and a quick vision of Mr. Darcy from *Pride and Prejudice* asking me to dance floated through my brain. And then my little fantasy popped like a soapy bubble landing on the lawn. Alice was staring at me.

"It's beautiful," I whispered.

Alice opened the box.

"Oh no- don't!" I said, afraid all the magic would disappear once the box was open.

"Well- let's see how well preserved this thing is."

The dress was even more beautiful out of the box. It didn't look like a wedding dress; it didn't look like a prom dress. It was the most romantic dress I had ever seen in my entire life.

Alice put the dress in my hands, but I didn't know what to do with it, so I carefully slid my fingers tips up and down the length of the long skirt, fingering little bits of the embroidery.

"Do you want to try it on?"

"Oh no… wait can I?"

"Yes, there's a mirror up here. Throw your clothes on top of that trunk and you can change up here. I'll be back in about ten minutes- I need to make a phone call before the pharmacy closes. There's a hat up here too, somewhere. I doubt you'll want the hat, but we can look for it when I come back. I'll tell Martin what you are doing, so he doesn't come up here and peek."

I was so excited; I had my shirt off even before Alice hit the first step to go downstairs. Fumbling at first with the zipper, I had to tell myself to relax and breathe so I wouldn't tear the dress or zipper. The dress slipped over my head and fit- it was a miracle. For several long sweet minutes I pictured myself dancing with Martin while wearing the dress and it was like being dropped right in the middle of a Jane Austen novel.

But I knew I couldn't wear it to the prom, it was his mother's wedding dress and that was weird. Not ready to take it off though, I took my time enjoying how it felt to have it on. I twirled around in the mirror several times to look at the back, and then I remembered the hat.

There were a lot of cardboard boxes in the attic, but most of them were labeled and if the labels were accurate they were obviously not what I was looking for. I turned to the steamer trunk that I put my clothes on and opened the trunk.

A pink hat sat right on top of the contents inside the trunk. I picked it up and put it on my head before looking at it in the mirror. It was a large, jaunty spring hat made of raffia. I liked it, but wasn't sure what to do with it because it didn't quite go with the dress. Putting the hat back in the trunk, I glanced over the rest of the contents.

Besides the hat, there were a few small boxes with letters and pictures inside. They were mementos from Martin's dad. I was curious about Martin's dad, but didn't want to intrude on Martin and Alice in a personal way that they hadn't yet shared with me. Neither one of them ever mentioned Martin's father. I wasn't sure if Alice was divorced or widowed.

At the very bottom of the trunk was a long metal box with a sturdy combination padlock. The metal lock box intrigued me more than the open cardboard boxes of letters and pictures. Holding the box in my hands, I was met with a faint humming. Not exactly the same buzzing I heard if someone died, but a strange feeling came over me as I held the box. Not thinking, but rather feeling my way, I put my hands carefully on the padlock and felt the recessed numbers.

5-27-4

The numbers spoke to me as if making dull impressions on my fingertips. I turned to the number five right; twenty-seven left; and four to the right and snapped open the lock. Inside the box was a certificate with writing on it in a foreign language and an old fur cape wrapped in a dry cleaner's bag.

I wasn't familiar with furs; the only ones I had ever seen were at the estate sales I went to with my mother on the weekends. Some of the fur coats they sold at these sales were horribly old and falling apart. Most of them reeked of cigarettes and had lipstick stains on the lining. Every last bit of glamor the furs held had dried up long ago. But this little fur was different- the skin was still surprisingly supple and it had a pleasant odor when I slid it out of the plastic. Strangely, I found myself putting the fur to my face to experience the softness of the hair and to breathe in the scent.

The fur smelled like sea water and sunlight, wrapped in a downy softness I had never felt before. As I breathed in the scent, I felt uncertain. Shouldn't this dead thing make me feel uncomfortable and trigger a little bit of my banshee instinct, even though it was just a piece of old clothing? After all, this animal was once alive. In it I sensed residual warmth in the pelt as if the animal fur was not so dead and there was a small fragment of life yet in it.

Suddenly, realizing that I had broken open a locked box, I quickly folded the cape back into the box and stuck it back in the trunk. I rearranged the boxes of letters and pictures on top of the metal box and finally placed the raffia hat inside on top of everything.

Alice called from the foot of the stairs, "are you okay Sinead?"

"Yes- I'm coming, just a minute."

I quickly took the dress off and put my clothes back on. Then I carefully refolded the wedding dress and placed it back in the box. The seal on the box to preserve the dress had been broken so I brought it back down with me so Alice could put it somewhere for safe keeping or seal it up again before storing it back in the attic.

"So what do you think?"

"I love it," I said.

"Does it fit?"

"Yes- I need to find something like it online."

"Why can't you wear my dress? Don't feel weird about it being a wedding dress; it wasn't originally made for a wedding. No one will guess it was worn at my wedding, it came from a thrift store."

It took a few moments for what she said to sink in. "I can wear it. Wow!"

I hugged Alice crushing the box between us. "Wait a minute; won't Martin think it's strange for me to wear his mom's wedding dress to the prom? It might seem like I am jumping the gun or something…"

"Why tell him it's my old wedding dress? He wasn't there- he wouldn't know the difference."

"Won't he recognize it from pictures of you and his dad?"

"No! There aren't a lot of those around. I'll stick it in my bedroom and I can drop it off at your house later. There's no reason for him to know that it was a wedding dress or where it came from for that matter. Did you find the hat?"

"Yes. It's still upstairs; I put it back in the trunk. I didn't think you would let me wear your dress."

"In the trunk?" asked Alice. She frowned and stiffened up for a second. "I'll put this on my bed and go get the hat too."

She stuck the presentation box on the foot of her bed, before closing the door to her bedroom. The attic stairs were still down and Alice went up them. I followed behind her just onto the stairs, but didn't go up into the attic. Sticking my head through the opening in the floor, I watched as Alice opened the trunk.

The pink hat sat on top of the boxes of letters and pictures where I left it. Alice moved slowly as if inspecting something before picking up the hat.

"I didn't look in the boxes," I blurted out.

"Of course not, I know you're not nosy. Anyway there's nothing to see," said Alice. "Martin's dad has been gone for a long time," she added.

Alice took the hat out and then carefully rearranged the boxes back in the steam trunk. I couldn't tell for sure, but I thought she picked up the metal box too. The padlock clanged softly against the box as Alice adjusted things.

She was quiet, but when Alice turned around she was smiling. I wanted to ask her about the glamorous little fur cape too, it would look great worn over the dress, but I held my tongue. The box was obviously locked and I didn't want her to think badly of me for picking the lock. Or think I was a thief.

I smiled back at Alice and walked backwards down the steps. I was beaming since I had the perfect dress. I could relax- the dress from Alice was even better than the one I picked out online and I didn't even have to pay for it. I was so excited- this was going to be a prom to remember.

CHAPTER 12

For weeks, it felt like I was being watched. I had the strongest sensation I was never alone and then just as the feeling became unbearable it ended.

Spring can be miserable in Sheboygan. It's a long wait for winter to end punctuated by drippy, watery days chased by bone chilling winds off Lake Michigan. Martin and I spent most of that damp spring indoors, either swimming at the Road Inn on the weekends or nursing hot coffee at Paradigm after school.

It was only at Paradigm that I thought of Kelly and our long talks. I remembered how she would take me there for human comforts when I needed it; for warmth, food, something hot to drink, and a quiet spot to talk on a cozy couch. And sometimes when I sat there with Martin, flush from being near him, I remembered how different Kelly smelled- unlike humans; she was icy and intoxicating. There was a freshness to her that was like a predatory flower. She was a Venus flytrap waiting for me to get to close enough before she concealed me in her sharp embrace.

One unusually dry afternoon, Martin and I sipped our coffees, watching the shadows creep up the windows at twilight. Indistinct figures walked by from time to time peeking in at the people nestled in intimate formations. I had that watched feeling again.

"I have to go, my mom will kill me if I'm late," Martin said as he put his mug down on the table.

He kissed me slowly, before walking out the front door. I jumped up to go home too, before it got cold and dark. I still didn't like to walk home alone after being attacked by vampires. Putting our empty mugs in the bin on the front counter, I zipped my coat and left behind him. I wouldn't try to catch up to Martin, because he had a dinner date with family, it would be enough to follow him at a distance. There was safety in his shadow, even from a block away.

Outside in the cool air, the feeling of being watched was gone. Sometimes it felt like my mind was playing tricks on me, because the feeling was so intense that it was like being under a spotlight. And it was strange how the *watched* feeling came and went- like someone turned it on and off like a light switch.

Down the street, Martin was a tiny point in the distance. A dark silhouette lingered in the covered parking lot of the funeral chapel across the street. It was a familiar shape, but I couldn't see very well as night fell. And then the figure stepped out of the shadows, crossed the parking lot and stood motionless in the alley.

It was Kelly. I wanted to get her attention but something stopped me. She was deep in thought and watching someone. She was like a cat hunting, the way she was poised behind the funeral home. With a slight twitch, Kelly resumed moving and glided down the street.

The way Kelly walked reminded me of how Marney and Gregory walked when they escorted me across the railroad tracks to kill me.

Kelly was following Martin. And when I realized it, I followed her from a safe distance all the way to his house. When Martin went inside, shutting his front door, Kelly paused briefly before she headed back towards downtown.

Continuing to follow her, I put plenty of room between her and me, as she walked back to Paradigm. Kelly was obviously coming back to look for me, but then at the last minute she ignored the coffee shop completely and slipped inside an apartment building across from the funeral home. I was confused.

After I was certain Kelly was inside one of the apartments, I went to the front door and tried it. It wasn't locked, and it opened exposing a narrow strip of dirty carpeted stairs that led to the apartments upstairs and five metal mailboxes at the foot of the stairs.

Three of the mailboxes were labeled with names on them that I didn't recognize. Sliding my hand over the first of the two unlabeled mailboxes- the locked box opened for me. The box contained a couple pieces of junk mail addressed to someone- not Kelly. That left the box for apartment number four and it was empty.

I had found Kelly's new home. A vampire doesn't receive mail; no personal letters, or junk mail and certainly not bills. It's as if they were dead, if you judged by the amount of snail mail they received.

So Kelly was back- but her return home was not like I expected. Why was she avoiding me? If I asked her directly about it, it would be like it was in the past. Kelly only told me what she wanted to- when she was good and ready to tell me. But I needed to know what was going on, because something wasn't right.

There were so many unanswered questions, when it came to Kelly. That was the major problem with our relationship. Having her as a best friend left me closed off from so many mysterious secrets. I guess it couldn't be helped with her being a vampire- that was how she protected me from her world. But for me there was never any comfort in secrets. A secret was just a hidden, inconvenient truth. I could deal with the truth out in the open, even if it was uncomfortable or painful.

That's when I decided I would break into her apartment.

I closed the door behind me quietly and went back to Paradigm. Calling my mom from my cell phone I told her I would be late, and then sat down in a window seat facing Kelly's apartment building and ordered another coffee.

The coffee was a bad choice, because I had to pee before finishing it. I worried that if I left to use the bathroom I would miss Kelly leaving. I had to be certain Kelly was gone before I entered her apartment. Kelly was my friend- but it would be like walking into a lion's den without a gun.

Sitting with my legs crossed tightly, I wasn't sure I really wanted to sneak in to her apartment. Wouldn't it be easier to walk up to her front door and knock? I could tell Kelly that I saw her leaving earlier when Martin left Paradigm. Only I wouldn't mention that I saw her stalking my boyfriend.

Just when my bladder was about to burst and I was dangerously close to leaving a big wet spot on the couch, a light shut off in one of the upstairs windows across the street. The same window cracked open slightly and Kelly peered from behind the glass before she subtly changed into a shadow and exited through the open crack. Kelly had left the building to hunt for the night. Thankfully, I got to use the bathroom before something embarrassing happened. I emptied my bladder in the restroom before leaving to sneak into her apartment.

Breaking into number four was easy- Kelly didn't lock the front door. Inside her apartment, I didn't know what to expect, in the past I only imagined how the other half lived, since Kelly never invited me home.

The apartment was a dark and sparsely furnished one bedroom that was lacking any personal touches. The kitchen was spotless and Kelly probably never set foot in there. The refrigerator wasn't even plugged in.

There was a small bathroom off the single bedroom that appeared unused as well. In the bedroom, the bed was tightly and neatly made, and I suspected that Kelly rarely used it. There wasn't a coffin either; vampires didn't sleep in coffins with their native soil covering them. If they did rest it was in regular beds, but not for long. Resting was more of a mental break than physical need for vampires, or so I had been told. Besides the bed, the only thing of interest in the whole apartment was a small writing desk against the back bedroom wall. I opened all of the drawers in the desk and found most of them empty.

The bottom drawer held a small black book and a few nib pens. Soon I held Kelly's journal in my hands. I had seen her with at school many times. Once I even asked her if she was worried that a human would find it and read it… but she wasn't concerned with being exposed as a vampire. Who would believe it was anything more than a work of fiction anyway?

I had never peeked into her journal before. This was a huge violation of privacy, but I had to know, if I could, what was going on? This was as close as I could get to reading her mind. My heart pounded in my chest as the book fell open.

Flipping to the beginning I skimmed over an early entry; it was right after Marney had attacked Kelly and it was written in her beautiful Edwardian cursive.

I will never forgive myself for those two. Even now as I sit in Phoenix a sea of humanity reminds me of my last victims. The terror in the man's eyes as the life ebbed out of him was horrible. I hoped it would satisfy my thirst for some time but it was only an hour later that I found myself repeating the madness and searching out another victim.

My stomach dropped, Kelly was drinking human blood again after decades of abstaining. As her best friend, I was sympathetic because I knew how traumatic Marney's attack was. I was there for the aftermath and had lived through a similar attack. But the part of me that had an aversion to vampires and knew Kelly was dangerous was horrified.

Overwhelmed with fear, I wanted to drop the journal like a hot potato and run! Run home and hide like I did when I knew Marney was coming after me. But I swallowed my fear and read more, because I needed to know what the hell was going on. Kelly always kept me in the dark, but whether it was to protect me or not anymore- I was having serious doubts.

I held the book as if it could scorch me. Landing in the middle of the handwritten journal- I flipped past the early entries and read. There was a brief entry about her coming to visit me in the night. So I hadn't dreamed it. And there was another short entry about how I was unhappy with Martin.

The jealous female inside me pricked up when I saw Martin's name written in her precise old fashioned handwriting. I flipped through the pages looking for his name specifically and didn't have far to look; all the most recent entries were about Martin.

Kelly had been watching us swimming at Road Inn on the weekends- or rather she had been watching Martin. Not only that- but this wasn't the first time she had followed him. She was making sure he was going home alone. I understood then, why the watched feeling came and went so dramatically.

There was more… Kelly knew Martin was a virgin and she wanted to make sure he remained that way. Secretly- I was glad to read that Martin was still a virgin, but it disturbed me insanely that Kelly knew a lot of very private details about Martin. What else did she know about my boyfriend?

It was obvious she had been reading Martin's mind and that bothered me even more than her reading my mind. I was pretty sure my boyfriend's mind, should be off limits to other girls! Kelly was frightening me, and making me angry. Not only had she been drinking human blood again- she was in love with my boyfriend!

The rest of Kelly's journal was a horror story. In it she described her intense love and longing for Martin. And she wrote about how she had changed her mind about me. She had a sick theory, that I wasn't a banshee- a harbinger of death, but rather a siren that bended the will of men for my own personal use. Kelly believed that I made Martin unhappy. And if he got away from me, and out from under my spell, he could find happiness in a relationship with her. And the best way for them to be in a relationship was for Kelly to make him a vampire. In that way they could be a couple forever.

Kelly's sudden love for Martin had turned into jealousy and hatred towards me since I was with him. She wanted to hurt me, like she had been hurt by Marney. She knew how much prom meant to me and she would defeat me then. She would change Martin into a vampire on the night of the prom and take him away from me. But Kelly wouldn't kill me; instead she would take pity on me because we were once friends.

I stood there in shock. Beads of sweat pooled on my forehead. I dropped her journal on the floor before my sweat rubbed off onto the fragile ink. Holding the book by the corner, I threw it back into the bottom drawer, and wondered if I could get away with barfing in her bathroom without her finding out. No- she would smell me.

My life had just run out.

I couldn't understand her new twisted vampire morality. She was crazy, something had snapped inside her. I had to stop her.

And there was only one good way to stop a vampire. You didn't reason with vampires and you couldn't lock them in a cell for eternity. An agreement with a vampire was obviously subject to change on their part. The only way to stop a vampire permanently was to kill it.

I would have to kill Kelly. And I knew the method I would use. I thought back to that awful day when Marney, Paul, and Gregory came after me. I knew for certain after watching Rex stake Paul and Gregory that there was a sure fire method to kill a vampire and grind them into the dust. I would have to stake her.

Kelly was strong and she could read my mind so this wouldn't be easy. But there were two things that could work to my advantage. If Kelly was focused on Martin she wouldn't read my mind and find out that I was going to kill her. She would never suspect me.

The other thing was that I had supernatural strength when I was a banshee that was even hard for her to overcome. Kelly struggled to hold me down, the night Marney attacked her. The trick would be how to transform right when I needed the strength to overcome her.

There was nothing left for me here, I gathered what little resolve I had dropped on the floor of her apartment and sneaked out the back. I was deeply worried and on the verge of hysterics.

The prom was in a few days, and I still didn't know how I would stake Kelly. It's not like I could just walk up to her and push a stick into her chest. Finally- I decided to make a stake first and then work out the details later.

Borrowing a wooden baseball bat from school, I stashed it in my basement. No longer concerned with color coordinating accessories with Alice's dress, I worked on my new project for junior prom, shaving the bat down with my dad's power sander until I had a formidable stake.

After making it, I still had no idea how I would use it on Kelly though. In the movies, the vampire hunter follows the vampire in the early morning hours to their coffin. When it is finally daylight and the vampire is sleeping, the vampire killer opens the coffin and stakes the lethargic blood sucker.

This would never work in real life. Vampires could be out in the sunlight and they didn't sleep in coffins either. I knew about the coffins, because Kelly had shared some of her personal habits with me. Vampires were only lethargic when they hadn't drank enough blood and unless I could find a way to starve her, Kelly would be energetic and full of vampire fight when I went at her.

As for sneak attacking Kelly while she slept, vampires did need rest, but creeping up on her in her sleep wouldn't work. Vampires were super sensitive when humans were around them whether or not they were asleep.

I needed help, but if I asked Martin to help me kill Kelly, he would have me committed. He disliked Kelly, but not to the point of killing her. The only person I knew who could help me get the job done was Rex. I still had his phone number, but it was laughable to ask him to help me kill Kelly, since he was her friend. If I called Rex, he would show up at my door and help himself to my blood.

What I needed was a vampire hunter, but I wouldn't find one online.

I fired up my laptop turning to it for answers like I did when I wanted to know about banshees. In seconds, I found what I was looking for. The internet described many methods of killing vampires, and even went into great detail about staking vampires. But these descriptions were all written by people who thought vampires only existed in books and movies. They made it seem as easy as… as easy as bludgeoning a baby seal.

That's when my mind started going off in other directions. It wasn't hard to distract myself from the gruesome deed I was contemplating. When my mind went into overdrive, I let it wander to other things. I checked my email and played a video game online. The stress was killing me.

Closing my eyes, I listened to a haunting Celtic melody. I meditated on it and let it linger until it burst open with a vivid seascape on the horizon of my consciousness.

In the cold water of the Atlantic Ocean a small seal, darted and dived, playing with the currents, and rushing between rocks and crevices. The small creature should have been tucked away in a sheltered shore asleep, but like most young creatures, nighttime was an irresistible lure for exploring, especially when adults were sleeping.

The tiny seal made a final playful leap in the water and pulled himself back on land, but the beach he landed on, this landscape was unfamiliar. There were no seals sleeping and no familiar smells or sounds of snoring kin, only the sound of the ocean lapping the shore around him. And without thinking about consequences the small seal did the one thing he should have never done. He went behind the large rocks, shed his skin and returned to explore the beach walking upright as a human being.

The moonlight illuminated each of the boy's silent footsteps as he explored the beach for treasure and enjoyed the sensation of being human. The selkie child was unafraid as he walked on land. The humans wouldn't harm him as they might have if he remained a seal.

In the distance a small shack of stone and wood stood, the only structure for miles. Inside it an old fisherman dozed in noisy slumber under a blanket of three dispatched pints of lager. Entering the shack, the young boy stared at the sleeping man with reverence and curiosity, before looking through the sea shanty for curious objects and treasure to take back with him to the sea.

When the man woke startled, his blood shot eyes focused on the boy and he grabbed the thief. But he recognized the naked boy for what he was and covered the boy with a blanket and kept him in the shanty until the early dawn. And at day break the old man covered the boy with a clean flannel shirt and then took the young boy back to the beach to find his shed skin. But after many hours of searching and turning up nothing, the man believed the tide had swallowed the boy's pelt.

My head jerked and hit the desk; a thin string of drool attached my chin to the laptop like fishing line. I wiped a pool of spit off my keyboard with my sleeve and frantically changed my internet search.

My mind was really working in another direction. This dream wasn't a dead end like the one with the old crone; this dream had a spark of truth in it. Martin was a supernatural being. Why else was I so attracted to him, despite his indifference to me at times?

Several elements of his personality started to make sense; besides his amazing swimming skills and love of the water, like how he had a distant, melancholy attitude towards life- as if he didn't fit in either.

After I woke up, I knew that only a fraction of my dream was true, and that many of the details had been supplied by my subconscious. So I tried to piece together what was true.

For one thing, I knew where the seal skin was. It was certainly not lost. Alice had Martin's skin tucked away in a locked metal box in her attic. She was the one who made a selkie her son, keeping him away from his previous life in the ocean. No wonder Alice hated swimming season. Martin was so gifted and at home in the water that it threatened her happy home with her son.

My focus switched from killing Kelly, to doing the right thing for Martin. I needed to rescue Martin from his current captor, his adopted mother. Not just rescue him from Kelly who wanted to enslave him by making him a vampire. If I could return Martin's pelt to him, maybe I wouldn't need to kill Kelly. With Martin gone, maybe whatever anger and bitterness she felt towards me would disappear. If not, I would cross that bridge when I got to it. That night I knew- that no matter how this turned out, I would be losing my boyfriend forever.

The next step was getting back into Alice's attic. I had to be extremely cautious in proceeding, because Alice wouldn't let her adopted son go easily. If Alice suspected what I was doing, would she destroy his pelt?

Wondering why his mother kept his seal skin instead of destroying the pelt to keep Martin from returning to the sea, I looked it up on the internet. I was sure I already knew the answer, but to be sure I checked.

Burning or destroying a selkie's pelt would kill a selkie.

Was it possible Alice might destroy the skin rather than lose her son forever? Sometimes, I doubted Alice's motherly instincts. But if she truly loved Martin and didn't want any harm to come to him, she would never destroy his skin. And then I would only need to retrieve his skin and return it to him.

It sounded simple, but there were so many things to consider. I had to make sure that Alice didn't catch on to me or she would hide the pelt again- this time where it would never be found.

There was also Kelly. What would she do if she found out Martin was a selkie? And that I was returning his seal skin to him so he could return to the ocean. It was a problem knowing Martin was a selkie, since Kelly could read my mind. I would have to avoid her at all costs. Not only would my plans fail if she knew about Martin, I would be in deep trouble if she found I was going to put a stake through her heart.

Besides those two female landmines to maneuver, there was Martin. Did he know his true nature? What if he didn't want to go back to the ocean? And what body of water could Martin return to?

Fortune smiled on me; the giant lake near our house would be the key to getting Martin back home to the ocean. He could use Lake Michigan to return to the Atlantic Ocean. It would be difficult for him- but it could be done. He could navigate Lake Michigan, then lakes Huron and Erie, next Lake Ontario and finally the St. Lawrence Seaway once he was a seal.

I emotionally distanced myself from Martin. With only a week until junior prom, our time together was coming to a close. I would still act happy and excited about the prom, just as I had before I knew Kelly was scheming to turn Martin into a vampire. But inside of me the weight of the world rested on my shoulders.

What would happen to all of us- if I was not able to change the course we were on? We were on opposing paths, getting ready to collide and Kelly had the upper hand.

Martin was in the water, the dim lights of the pool making shadows where he swam at high speeds for an impossible amount of time underwater. He was no longer a shark in the water; he was so much more vulnerable. In the deep water, he was a seal.

"Aren't you coming in?"

"No, not this time, I don't feel well Martin."

"C'mon on, you can't just sit there and watch me swim…"

"I feel like I'm catching a cold or something. I don't think I should get in, I don't want to get sick before prom."

He understood and ducked back under the water for a few more turns.

"Hey, does that mean no kissing?" Martin asked as his head emerged at my feet.

"For now."

"Hmmm- I'm going to have a lot to look forward to Friday night. You better feel well by then."

He didn't know the half of it.

AN UNLUCKY CHAPTER 13

Watching her breathe and dream in the middle of the night was supposed to comfort me and calm my persistently agitated state. My conscience had sent me to her in one last ditch effort to make me change my course.

At first I simply watched her sleep, but as the night unfolded, I tried to read her subconscious mind something I had refrained from in the past.

Her mind wasn't an open book like most human minds. Half human, half supernatural minds are different. They're harder to read because in the supernatural mind the conscious and subconscious flows together in a more fluid motion as if there is no separation between the two thought processes. It's an art to reading this type of mind, distinguishing between what is the truth and what is fantasy. The subconscious is a murky, difficult landscape to maneuver anyway and one should be careful about drawing a conclusion when exploring another person's mind.

Dreams materialized and dematerialized, there were no nightmares yet, but Sinead was obviously troubled. The water and a lost boy was a major theme running through her mind. It was nothing that interested me. But just as I was about to leave her in peace to dream alone, I saw something troubling on the horizon.

A nightmare was taking shape that was based in part on both the recent past and a future plan. Sinead was backed against a wall, a vampire pinning her in a final haunting embrace. Marney was about to sink her teeth into Sinead, and I watched transfixed unable to pry myself out of Sinead's dream. I was horrified at her demise and yet thrilled by the blood about to be spilt.

The vampire bent in- her teeth sinking into Sinead's neck. Blood would flow. But blood didn't just ebb and flow, it leaked out of the vampire who was feeding too fast to contain it. And blood spilled out over the gluttonous vampire. The fool must have already gorged herself before feeding. What a waste!

Finally- the vampire fell back from Sinead's neck and I gasped! The creature was not Marney, it was me! Blood stained the front of my shirt and it soaked the ground. The vampire was not gorged; Sinead had staked me in the heart. I lay dying for an instant, before smoldering into the ground, and becoming one substance with the dirt.

Sinead's subconscious was not disturbed. This was not a nightmare for her, but a plan made and what she hoped would be the outcome. I had a glimpse of what she had in store for me in the future.

Stopping her would be easy; I could have taken her life right then if I wanted to. But easy wasn't fun. I liked to play with my food before eating. In the beginning, Sinead had been appalled by my predatory nature. I once ran from my primitive nature too, but no longer. I would enjoy every moment that led up to the end of Sinead.

I had so much to look forward to on prom night.

CHAPTER 14

I was dreading prom night so much that I neglected to get my hair and nails done or make any arrangements for myself. My mom must have noticed because she dragged me out of the house the day before prom to get a manicure and pedicure- even though sitting still long enough to get it done would be slow torture.

"Is anything wrong Sinead?" my mom asked on the drive over to the salon.

"No- I'm just nervous."

"I heard a lot about what happens at these proms."

"You mean drinking and losing my virginity?"

My mom choked slightly, but then maintained her composure. "Well, I wouldn't put it that bluntly, but I was thinking something along those lines."

"Well- don't mom; you don't have anything to worry about. I don't like drinking, it doesn't agree with me. It makes me sick."

I didn't tell her everything makes me sick- like turning into a banshee that howled in graveyards and being friends with a real vampire. And how about killing my best friend to keep her from stealing my boyfriend and making him a vampire? That would make anyone queasy- maybe even sick of life.

"That's good- I guess, I won't ask how you know about drinking. But if you do drink, please call me for a ride. No questions asked- okay? I don't want you to be afraid to call me if you get into a sticky situation of any kind."

"Thanks mom- will do." I smiled at her, but it looked forced and creepy when I saw my reflection in the side mirror.

She looked over at me with those eyes that had a half dozen unspoken questions.

"Mom don't worry about the other thing."

"Mm-hmm," she mumbled like she wasn't concerned and gripped the steering wheel until her knuckles turned colors.

"Martin isn't the one for me."

"How do you know?"

"He just isn't the one. I know it- for sure. I wouldn't be surprised if we broke up after prom," I added.

"Oh honey, is there something going on?"

"No mom, nothing is going on. It's just these things don't last forever. Not in high school," I shrugged like it was no big deal.

The manicure technician led me to a table and worked on my nails. I tried to relax and enjoy being pampered; having my nails done was a new experience. And the next time I got it done, it might be done by a mortician. While my nails were polished a rosy pink, I formulated a final plan of action and tried not to hyperventilate from sitting still for the first time in a week.

On the day of prom, I woke up while it was still dark outside. Going back to sleep was not an option, so I got out of bed and dressed in comfortable clothing. School was a half day for juniors and seniors and I would need the free afternoon to work through my plan. At noon, I would go straight to Martin's house for his seal skin. And after retrieving it, I would meet Martin at the lake and somehow convince him to leave before Kelly got involved.

To get Martin to the lake, I would imply that we were going to get romantic before prom. I hated to lie to him, but I couldn't think of anything else.

The bell rang dismissing the juniors and seniors at noon. Martin was waiting for me after school.

"I can't wait to see you tonight," he whispered in my ear.

"Me too," I said. "I'd like to meet you at the lake before prom."

"How come?"

"Because it would be romantic- we could watch the sunset and hang out alone before the dance starts."

"Where do you want to meet and what time?"

There were stars in his eyes, those little flickers of whimsy that break out in a man's eyes when he thinks he's going to get something...

"Meet me by the breakwater by the power plant around six pm."

"It's pretty isolated down there- are you sure?"

"Yeah, I'm sure. I want to be alone with you."

Martin smiled at me; I could tell he would be there... I knew exactly what was on his mind. Mind reading wasn't just for vampires.

Things were falling into place. If all went well, Kelly wouldn't try anything on Martin until later at the dance. I was one step ahead of her. If I could have gotten Martin's skin earlier, she wouldn't have a ghost of a chance. He would be long gone.

But this was the first time I would have a chance to get into his house. Martin was hanging with some guys from swim team until late afternoon and Alice would still be at work. It would take me less than twenty minutes to get into his house and into the attic. If all went well- I would call him to meet me earlier. There wasn't much that could go wrong.

Before leaving school, I emptied my backpack out into my locker so I could stash Martin's pelt inside. The only thing I left inside was the stake I made out of an old baseball bat. I hoped I wouldn't have to use it. The weight of it pressed into my left shoulder blade as I waited on the school steps until Martin left. Once he was out of sight I walked to his house, carrying the stake like it was a cross.

Martin's house was quiet when I peered into a back window. The back door was locked, but it opened, simply by me wishing it to open. Someday in the future when I had time, I would work on these new powers but it would have to wait.

I closed the back door softly and went to the hall. Pulling down the stairs, I climbed into the attic and immediately went to the trunk for the seal fur. Everything was as I last left it. The piles of letters and pictures stacked and organized in little boxes and the padlocked metal box at the bottom. Trying the same numbers again, the lock clicked open.

The box was empty!

It was obvious and yet I still ran my hand down the length of the box as if it weren't possible. Was Alice was on to me? Chills ran down my spine. I panicked, my plans were crumbling.

Quickly I put the box back into the bottom of the trunk and took a few deep breaths. Alice had obviously removed the seal skin as a precaution because I had been up here. I probably would have done the same if I was her.

I had boxes to check and a whole house to search. In the meantime it wasn't even one pm and I still had plenty of time to look before Alice would be home from work. Inhaling deeply, I shut out the voices that were telling me to panic and start throwing things around. Instead I started methodically opening boxes in the attic.

"What are you looking for?"

Kelly's voice dripped with menace. Turning to face her I edged the strap of my backpack down on my left side so I could quickly unzip my pack and arm myself.

"Oh Alice, It's only you. You scared the crap out of me."

She didn't say anything. Alice wore a crooked, fake grin that meant danger. I had seen it enough on Kelly's face to know what it meant.

"I was looking for the hat," I stammered. "I wasn't expecting you home."

"Oh, I see," she said slowly, "I always come home for lunch on Friday."

Alice was slow to speak and was thinking through her words. We would be playing a game of verbal chess. And if I stalled her long enough, before getting kicked out, I could still locate the seal skin. She was going to ask me to leave sooner or later, but I had to figure something out fast.

"How did you get in?"

"Hmmm- oh Martin let me in before he left with his friends. I told him I left something up here."

"The hat was it?"

"Yes."

"That's not possible, Sinead, I dropped the hat and dress off at your house."

Alice was right, my beautiful prom dress and the hat were on my bed where I left them this morning. I couldn't resist looking at the dress one more time before leaving for school.

"I must have lost the hat. I don't remember you bringing it over… so I assumed it was still up here in the trunk."

"You didn't come here for the hat, did you?"

I hadn't expected that, Alice cut to the chase and forced my hand. For a brief moment I wished she was a vampire. A vampire will toy with you and play with you a bit… this one she wanted everything out in the open. Changing tactics, I frowned and hung my head sheepishly. I wasn't a very good liar.

"Umm- no… I hate to admit it but I was snooping around."

"Well that's apparent."

"I saw the letters and pictures from Martin's dad and I wanted to look through them. I didn't mean to snoop honestly."

Adding the word honestly, was like putting cement shoes on, it made the lie only that much more obvious. The scent of lies and danger hung heavy in the air.

Alice lifted an eyelid at me in reproach and walked over to the trunk. She flicked the lid open like it was a pop can and looked at the boxes of letters and cards. It would have helped my case if I hadn't put them back in such an exact manner.

Blood rushed to my head and there was a buzzing noise. I tried to breathe deeply or else I would pass out. I was going banshee because she wanted to kill me. It seemed extreme, that she would be this calm and yet mad enough to kill.

"That's strange. Everything is still in the trunk. What are you really looking for?"

"That's it really- I just couldn't help snooping around up here. We don't have an attic with interesting stuff in it."

The buzzing noise was getting louder; it was an early warning that I was going to scream. It was the noise that tuned up a banshee's vocal chords; before cutting into a shriek that could shatter glass and eardrums.

She was going to kill me. She knew I came for the pelt... she was going to kill me! I repeated it over and over like a sick mantra.

I couldn't shut off the noise. Ripping open my backpack, I pulled out the stake I made for Kelly and flipped it upside down. And without thinking I pointed it at the top of Alice's head and swung, levitating and screeching in one gruesome action. As quickly as I screamed and hit her, I cut it off into a silent staccato. The last thing I needed was curious neighbors.

Alice was on the floor. She was dead or unconscious- maybe both. There was no way I was going to touch her to find out. I half wondered if she had a heart attack from seeing me change. Terror flickered in Alice's eyes just before I put her lights out. It wasn't a slight change from teenage girl to hovering; screeching banshee- it was like a bomb going off in a small space.

The buzzing was still strong in my head and made me nauseous to the point of vomiting, even though it was receding. I let myself down onto my feet lightly and stumbled down the stairs. Why was being a banshee so unpleasant... being a vampire, at least for Kelly, wasn't unpleasant? She seemed to enjoy drinking blood.

Outside, the fresh air was bringing me back to reality. I was at square one, but with a casualty. I had killed my boyfriend's mom. But what happened to Alice couldn't be helped and I needed to find his skin. After I reunited Martin with his skin, I could deal with the mess that was Alice. And deal with lawyers and prison sentences. This was not the time with Kelly still out there waiting for the moment to change Martin into a vampire.

Hope wasn't lost yet, Alice couldn't have destroyed the pelt or it would have hurt Martin and he was still fine as far I knew. I doubted that Alice moved the pelt much further than her house.

The buzzing was a faint ringing in my ears as I sat on the back steps. I noticed Alice had planted a lot of fresh flowers in the backyard. It was a grim and serendipitous moment when I found the spot where I would bury Alice later. Regaining my wits- I didn't plan on going to jail for murdering her. Fortunately Alice was in the attic, so I wouldn't have to move her until after I finished getting Martin back into his skin. And I was sure his skin was still in the house or the garage; or perhaps Alice had moved it to the basement.

By four in the afternoon, I was dirty and ready to admit defeat. I had carefully searched all the bedrooms and bathrooms. The basement was fairly empty to begin with, so it didn't take long to turn up nothing. In the garage I made one last ditch effort.

Alice's left her car keys on the kitchen counter and I used them to open her car trunk and search the car. The trunk was empty, except for a few dry-cleaning bags, and the garage was empty too. Alice was one of those rare people who used her garage for parking and not storage.

A dirty shovel was propped against a small potting table in the back. Empty containers of early spring bulbs littered the top. Picking up the shovel, I went to where the new plantings were in her garden and dug them up. After digging the shovel struck something soft and malleable a few inches below the roots and bulbs. A dry-cleaning bag poked out of the fresh earth, and I dropped the shovel and dug with my hands. Pulling the bag to the surface I recognized the fur that emerged. Alice had wrapped the selkie skin in dry cleaning bags and buried it beneath her flowers.

It didn't seem like the safest place to bury the selkie skin, but it fooled me. I wouldn't have given the flower beds a second thought, if I hadn't needed a place to bury Alice in the backyard. It was a happy accident that I had whacked Alice, because I finally had the pelt and the wheels of my plan were back in motion. Guilt would have to wait- it would hit me when I came back to bury her later.

Fishing Alice's car keys out of my pocket, I no longer needed a ride to the breakwater. I couldn't believe my luck as I stuffed Martin's furry seal skin into my backpack and threw it in the passenger seat. I could easily be to the other side of town and meet my boyfriend at the lake. In fact, I would be there before he was.

Grinding the clutch a few times, I was on the road, driving down Lakeshore Drive rehearsing words and phrases in my head. 'Goodbye, I'll miss you.' 'I love you, Goodbye.'

What if he didn't understand? What if the pelt meant nothing to him? Here strip down for me and put this fur on... before we do it. I tried not to laugh at my stupidity. I was trying hard to divert myself from what was really going on.

My heart was broken, I loved Martin, but I knew that it wasn't meant to be. This was the only way to stop Kelly from changing him into a vampire. The only way out was by returning him to the sea. He didn't belong to me or her, or his mother Alice. He belonged to something bigger and stronger then all of us, he belonged in the water. He belonged to her- he belonged to the ocean. That was the truth for him.

I remembered the words that Kelly once said to me when we talked about leaving my parents and my home.

When we were finally going to travel together in the future and I was afraid to leave.

Change is inevitable. I wasn't meant to be human, I'm a vampire now. I've been a vampire so long; sometimes I forget that I was human once. One day, you'll probably embrace being a banshee and leave behind the human part of you as well. Change hurts, but it can be good too.

Kelly felt being half human and half banshee was a liability. I knew she thought she could fix me by helping me become more of a banshee and less human. There were always people who liked absolutes. In their mind- you couldn't be one thing and another- you could only be just the one thing.

But I wasn't like that... I liked being a part of both worlds. I liked being human. I loved my parents and I loved Martin. And a part of me enjoyed being special, and being a banshee, despite the nuisance of changing- despite the uncomfortableness of being. But choosing one over the other would never be for me. I couldn't be fully human anymore and ditch my banshee nature. And just being a supernatural being or monster was wrong too, because it made a person lose their humanity. You only had to look at Kelly to see it was true.

What little humanity she had as a seed inside her was being watered and nurtured by her friendship with a human girl. And all the damage and suffering she felt was from supernatural creatures like her. We would never be the same again; our friendship would have to become human and deepen again or die.

Handing over Martin's selkie skin would close the doors on humanity for him. But it was better than letting him become a cruel beast like Kelly and Marney, or even Rex who had killed his own kind.

I didn't know how, but I would find a way to occupy both worlds. Maybe in prison I would have a lot of time to think about it. Maybe even write poetry and suffer for it.

The lot at the dog park was deserted when I parked Alice's car in the last space nearest to the bluff. This part of the beach was an isolated favorite with teenagers and solitude seekers. I slung my backpack over my shoulder for the last time and descended down the sandy path. The path at the end of the parking lot winded once through the tall bushes obscuring the beach and water below, and ended up at the breakwater.

People were in the water, I could hear them. It would be difficult for Martin and me to be alone. The water was choppy and I had seen the surfers flooding the harbor center as I drove this way. Martin would be coming down the path soon. So I would just have to make the best of it and find another secluded place away from the swimmers in wetsuits who were entering the surf at each of the breakwaters.

I should have peeked through the bushes before stepping out on the beach. Instead of coming upon another group of fresh water surfers, I was met with a horrifying scene. Martin had arrived earlier then I had anticipated. He was in the water swimming and he wasn't alone. A girl with long black hair was swimming and circling him, her arms around him.

Kelly had found out about our meeting at the breakwater! I was so concerned about her not reading my mind that it never occurred to me that she would read his. I should have realized that Kelly would follow him after school. And if she knew such intimate details as to the fact that Martin was still a virgin, he would be an open book to her. It never occurred to me that when I gave him a time and a place that I was setting an appointment for a trap that would be laid out for us.

I wanted to run, so I wouldn't see him changed. But something hard inside kept me walking to the water's edge. That hardness was my new killer instinct. Could Kelly sense how much I had changed in one short afternoon? Did she know what I had done… did she know I was just like her- a cold blooded killer?

My best friend and opponent smiled at me. And she had every reason to smile because she had already virtually won just by my showing up on the beach. But I wouldn't take defeat easily; I would look for an opening.

Kelly was manipulating Martin- that much was apparent. His back was to me and I was glad for that. I didn't want to see his face. I didn't want to see if he was feeling pleasure or pain from being in her clutches.

"Aren't you going to greet us?"

I would meet her taunts with silence. It was easier to think first and then react, if I didn't get pulled into a game of words. She wanted to play with me, instead of getting straight to business.

"No- I suppose not. It's probably pretty disappointing that you aren't going to have sex now and then walk arm in arm together all aglow to the prom."

I tried not to react, but vampires have a way with words that are disturbing and disgusting. Vampires always tried to break you, before they drained and killed you. It's in their nature, like a cat playing with a mouse.

"Well I couldn't let that happen now could I? I couldn't let my boyfriend lose it to you? That just wouldn't be right now, would it?"

Kelly had her legs wrapped around him, like a snake. She was squeezing him and writhing around him like a python asphyxiating a large meal.

For the second time in one day, the flies were buzzing. The swarming sound looped in my head, like a record track I couldn't turn off. I wanted to say something, but the buzzing prevented me from speaking.

Her intentions were clear- she was about to strike him at any second and here I was helpless to watch on the beach.

"Are you going to watch? Well than suit yourself!"

Kelly sneered at me and threw her head back. A canopy of sharp teeth angled out of her jaw and sunk into Martin as blood ran down his back. For the first time since I set foot on the beach, Martin moved. He struggled against her and she pulled him under the water, feasting and draining him. Martin choked and sputtered like a drowning victim, like someone who had never set foot in water before.

I tried to clutch something- anything to brace myself as my whole world turned upside down. Not only would I watch him die- I was going to announce Martin's death by screaming. In that final act I would be sounding the trumpet that said Kelly had won.

The noise gurgled up to my chest. In desperation I grabbed the stake from behind me and yelled the death knell.

The scream was wordless- but not meaningless. He's dying! Martin's dying! Those words were woven into my howls as I made the noise that only God and angels could decipher. It was the announcement of an impending death.

My body propelled across the water and I collided into them, going straight through them, because in my full banshee form I wasn't solid. The stake in my right hand was solid enough though and I thrust it into Kelly's chest with all the last of my mortal weight, before I became entirely ethereal and ghostlike.

The stake hit her squarely in the chest and Kelly screamed, loosening her jaws from Martin's neck wound. Blood poured out of her mouth, leaving a dark, filthy stain in the water. Hovering above the water I watched her terrified eyes as she sunk underwater.

Her eyes weren't dead eyes; they were the eyes of a frightened girl pleading for help. In an instant I was her friend again after landing the fatal blow. I wanted to reach underwater and pull her body to the surface, but in my present state I was just a being of light and particles.

My body was coming back to me and I needed to leave the water surface. I couldn't walk on water and I was far from the shore. Kelly kept sinking and I suddenly remembered Martin. Despite the lack of blood, Martin was swimming for the shore at Olympic speed.

Even from a hundred feet I could see he was a dead man. Blood was still trickling out of his collar bone where Kelly had bit into him and Martin was turning gray. I wanted to comfort him, but I was having a hard time moving through the air.

My open backpack was near where Martin landed on the beach. And he reached desperately for it to find something, anything to staunch the blood flowing from his neck. There was only one thing left in the backpack. And I was moved to tears as he unpeeled the fur from the dry-cleaning bag. Martin held it to his neck before collapsing into the sand to die.

I wasn't sure what I expected, but nothing happened. Martin hadn't changed into a selkie or a vampire even; instead he lay dying on the beach still in his withering human form.

As I got closer to the beach, I could feel my physical body return to me and I dropped into the water a few feet from the shore. The water was cold and jarring, but I was not prepared for what I saw next. Martin lay on the beach clearly gone, clutching the fur to his neck. Wading out of the water, I ran to him, throwing myself at his lifeless body. I cradled his motionless head in my lap and sobbed as he took a few more labored breaths. He turned a deeper shade of gray.

Why didn't the seal fur work? I pried the sticky cape off his neck and that's when I saw for the first time a vintage label sewn into the lining. The cape was just that, an old fur cape- there was nothing magical about it.

How could I be so stupid? I was so sure there was something supernatural about Martin. I was certain that he was a selkie and that his mother Alice had been hiding his seal skin in the attic. What else could explain how well he swam and how suspicious Alice had been when I was in her attic going through the steam trunk?

I had been wrong about everything. And everyone around me was dead. I had killed Alice and Kelly, and I had given Martin a death sentence too. I was so sure I could save him from being a vampire and he wouldn't even become that.

Martin stirred a little in my arms, he was still faintly breathing.

"Sinead, help me," he gasped.

"Martin?"

"I wanted to stay with you…"

"Stay with me, Martin. I need you."

"I can't, I'm dying, I thought I could stay- help me into the water."

"Are you a selkie?"

"No. Help me to the water, Sinead please." His eyes were going dark. His pupils were solid and dark, shark-like in death.

Confused, I started dragging him to the lake, because he could not stand and he was too heavy for me to carry him.

At the water's edge I dragged him in, still expecting him to turn into a seal and swim away from this awful place. When we reached the edge of the water and nothing happened, I wasn't sure what to do. He motioned for me to get closer to his face.

Leaning in, he whispered, "I love you."

"I love you too," I choked out- sobbing violently.

"I loved you the first night I saw you in the cemetery. You are a beautiful banshee."

I gasped; he had known who I was. How could I have been mistaken about him?

"Don't be afraid Sinead, pull me into the water."

I grabbed his feet and pulled. The water covered him; I was scared he would be fully covered and sink into the lake. I was afraid I would be drowning him, but he was dying anyway.

The water lapped at his chest, covering his neck and was up to his face. I watched how the water loved him. How any body of water wanted him, not just the sea. The water gently caressed his face and washed over his lips. And then it covered his nose. He wasn't breathing anymore- he was gone.

A terrific fear and anxiety engulfed my being as the waves finally covered him and he succumbed to the depths. I let go of his feet sobbing. His body was pulled away from me by the water that seemed alive and claiming its own. He sank deeper and deeper until there was no longer a glimpse of his body or even a shadow.

I stood in the water shaking.

Kelly and Martin were buried in the lake.

The sun was setting on this terrible day. Wave after wave hit me and I knew what I must do. I would throw myself into the lake too and be cleansed. I waded deeper into the water until the choppy waves hit me in the chest. A few more steps and I would be covered in the icy depths.

The water boiled and churned- angry at me for disturbing the tranquility of the day. And the lake gurgled and bubbled ready to claim one more victim.

A large shadow torpedoed towards me at high speed. It was too big for a seal, too big for a human or vampire; it was the size of a humongous, long oar boat. I wanted to turn and run, rather than be rammed by whatever was coming fast.

Suddenly, water rained down from above. I was soaked by a large shower of droplets. I looked up at the strange, cloudless rain shower- and stared into the face of a terrifying sea serpent! The monster's mouth gaping open to swallow me up. It let out a loud roar and I fell backwards before I could get a better look at the giant dragon that hovered above me.

Hitting the water, I fell silently to the earth hidden beneath the waves. The last thing I saw was the setting sun orange above me, as the water shimmered and twinkled illuminating a great beast from an ancient loch.

Voices called to me as I sunk.

Sinead... Sinead...

The three of us were buried at sea.

EPILOGUE

A dark figure whispered in the early morning hours. I managed a crooked smile at the monster at the foot of my bed and she smiled back at me, flashing a large set of teeth from under the veil of darkness.

"I'm alive?"

"Yes, of course, with barely a scratch on you. I pulled you out right away."

"How come you're not dead? I killed you."

"You have to hit my heart to kill me; you missed that by a mile…" It was not a mile; I would find out later that I had missed her heart by mere millimeters.

"I see."

"You're manipulating me now aren't you?"

I wasn't sure if it was the IV drip or her that made me calm despite what we had been through. It felt like there was a cold finger inside my skull massaging and calming my worried mind. There was that tendril in there that I recognized like the finger of God in my head. Only it wasn't God, it was just her, my personal demon I couldn't shake- my monstrous friend poking and rummaging around my brain trying to make me like her more than I already did.

"Yes, you could always tell," she whispered.

"Are you going to kill me now?"

"No." Kelly shook her head. She looked troubled, as if it was unbearable to her that I said it aloud. "I know it will take forever for you to trust me again. But for now it would be enough if you will have me near you again. Maybe one day you'll trust me. It's all I can hope for," she sighed.

"I never wanted to stop being friends" I said, "but I don't know if I can ever trust you again."

"I understand. But I never hurt you physically, just like I said. I would never hurt you- not your physical being. I never put my hands on you. It's something, right?"

"You don't think leaving me alone to deal with Marney and trying to change my boyfriend into a vampire could be misconstrued as hurting me?"

"You know what I mean, Sinead. I'm not perfect- I can't promise I will never hurt your feelings. Friends can try not to but it still happens. "

She was grasping at straws. Claiming that ace in the hole card, she waved it in my face- the fragile card that said, 'at least I never laid hands on you.'

"I know. Anyway I am in the same boat as you now."

"What do you mean?"

"I killed a person too."

"You mean Alice Cross?"

"Yes."

"She's not dead."

228

"Oh- well then she's probably going to kill me…"
I sighed. That would be one more thing to worry about
when the morphine stopped swallowing my emotions.

"I doubt it."

"Why's that? I took Martin away from her."

"That was going to happen anyway… that was a
long time in the making. I have already been to see her."

"You have? Where is she by the way?"

"In the hospital too, you knocked her out pretty
good, but she'll be discharged today. Before she got out I
reminded her that she tried to kill you first- if she tries to
contact you at all. She didn't seem too concerned about
you anyway; she just wanted to know where her son was."

"What did you tell her?"

"I told her that Martin left to be with his dad… that
he took off after the drama. His girlfriend beat up his
mother. It's in the newspaper."

I winced when she said that. I didn't understand
any of what had happened to Martin and Alice Cross.
Alice was alive; I hadn't killed her, so that was good.
Maybe I wouldn't go to jail for too long. And as for
Martin he wasn't a selkie, instead he was a horrible sea
serpent like something from out of Loch Ness.

"What did she say to that?"

"She's leaving town as soon as she gets out of the
hospital. If she stays around here, she'll end up in prison.
Sinead- she kidnapped Martin from his father. It was

inevitable that she and Martin would be split up. It was coming and soon."

"What?"

"Alice took Martin from his dad when he was a baby without a court order. Didn't you ever wonder why she hated it when Martin competed in swimming?"

"Umm- I thought it was because she knew he was a selkie. But I was so wrong about that- so I guess you'll have to explain it- why?"

"Because he was so good at it, he was in the local newspapers. And later if he swam in college or maybe the Olympics, Martin's biological father would probably read about it and find out where his son was."

"Oh, I see. So Alice was worried about me going through her papers and finding out she kidnapped Martin, and not about me getting my hands on that stupid fur cape. I feel so stupid about the cape."

"Why, Sinead? You knew Martin was a water changeling. He just wasn't a selkie. You're instincts for recognizing the supernatural around you are better than mine."

"Yes, I guess so. But if I wouldn't have gone after that cape, I would have never hit Alice and almost killed her. I wouldn't have even gone over there if I knew he wasn't a selkie. "

"But you did and you were marvelous. You knew you had to get him to a body of water so he could change back and you had to rescue him from me...," she trailed off.

"I don't want to talk about him much anymore, it's best to just forget and move on- he wasn't the one for me."

"Nor for I."

"You could have had me fooled; you wanted to make him into your vampire soul mate!"

"He wasn't my soul mate, I was just acting foolishly. Now I realize some of the contributing factors to my madness. I have a confession to make."

"I know... you've been drinking human blood again."

"How'd you know? Never mind. Yes, I did after Marney attacked me. It made me crazy. Having not been drinking human blood for so long, I couldn't take it. It didn't agree with me. I am not meant to drink human blood."

"That's refreshing to know."

"I can't explain away my bad behavior, Sinead. But I promise you if you give me one more chance it will be worth it. And you can trust me in the future. Not just for your physical safety but I don't want to hurt you emotionally either.

"Part of my problem, is I don't act like an adult. I act too much like a kid, and not a responsible one at that. I was made a vampire while my brain was still developing. Chronologically my brain may be a kid's brain, but I have almost a hundred years of life experience. You know, I'm not even sure if it's that… I haven't been acting like a kid; I've been acting like a fool."

I didn't interrupt her. I wasn't exactly innocent of acting foolish. I winced every time I thought about Alice and the *selkie* skin in her attic.

"As for Martin, I couldn't figure out why he was so attractive to me. But now that he's gone I think it had to do something with him being half human and half animal to some extent. I am a vampire; changelings are an exotic treat to me."

I made a face at her, despite Martin not being 'the one' he still was my boyfriend and she tried to steal him from me. I didn't want to hear that he was an 'exotic treat' to my best friend.

"I'm sorry- I don't want to make you uncomfortable. I am just trying to explain it all away I guess."

"Well you're not trying very hard. I did love him a little."

"Yes- you did and that's why I want you to know these things. I didn't love him, I wanted to drink his blood and make him into a trophy by changing him into a vampire. I'm sorry I tried to hurt you Sinead."

"It's okay."

What else could I say? The truth was I wanted to forgive her. I wanted to go back to our fantastic, magic carpet ride. I wanted to be her sidekick; I wanted to figure out how to control being a banshee. I didn't want us to end- especially not over a boy. And not one who was a freaking sea monster.

"No it's not okay. I was going to come here and pretend like what I did was no big deal because no one got killed. I was going to persuade you that everything was okay. Use my mind control on you- bend you to see things my way. But the truth is I tried to hurt you, and not because of who you are or anything you did. I wanted to hurt someone because of Marney and because I was disappointed with myself. And somehow that translated into me wanting to hurt you. I don't know how the lines could become so blurred..."

"We shouldn't try to figure it out. You're a vampire, I'm somewhat human. Vampires hunt humans. It's hard for you to go against your natural instincts, but you continue to try because you value our friendship. With practice it will get easier. It is what it is."

I didn't want to analyze things or try to figure them out. For the first time since the beginning of this horrible school year, I was at peace. Maybe it was the drugs talking, but all was well. Alice was leaving town, Marney was long gone, and Kelly was back to sitting on my bed talking to me and I knew she would try to make it up to me. And even Martin gone and never seeing him again made sense to me. I didn't have to look with trepidation towards some future date that held a long awful goodbye as we stopped being in love. And I didn't have to deal with the pain of seeing him with somebody else.

"I don't know if I really loved Martin. Maybe I just didn't want to see him with someone else," I said.

"No, you loved him. If you didn't- you wouldn't have tried to rescue him from me. You put yourself in a lot of danger from Alice and me, just to do the right thing for him. That's true love. And it's nothing short of noble and courageous. I wish I was more like you."

My cheeks blushed, sometimes the best part of Kelly was just listening to her speak, and not the magical things she did for me as a vampire.

"Kelly- one thing I don't understand is why Alice buried that fur cape. She had it under lock and key and then she buried it in her garden when she suspected I was snooping around."

"Alice hid the missing child report and the newspaper clippings of her kidnapping Martin in the lining of that cape. Alice thought you were on to her, that somehow you found out she took Martin from his dad on the internet. That's why she buried it, so if you kept digging around in the attic you wouldn't find anything up there.

"I gave this information to the district attorney's office. When you're better they'll want to talk to you, but you aren't in trouble. They're looking for Alice, not you. As far as they're concerned you two got in a fight because you found out Alice kidnapped Martin."

"Here- I don't know why, but I brought you this…" Kelly handed me the fur cape.

There was a large blood stain on the lining and the seams had been ripped open. Pressing the fur to my face, I smelled the sea again. I wanted to cry, but I knew that Kelly and the morphine were preventing me from sobbing even a little bit. There would always be time to cry about Martin later.

Sleep was coming for me again. I couldn't escape the clutches of slumber while Kelly manipulated my mood. She was making the room unnaturally peaceful and I was basking in the glow like a small lizard on a big rock under an artificial light. Her light was an artificial light I liked to bask in.

"I'm going to make this up to you."

"I know you will but how?" I said drifting in and out of conscious.

"I'm going to take you on that trip around the world, to find out who you are. Besides we need a good adventure for once. Not this silly amateur stuff we do around here like sleight of hand and scaring the pants off our peers."

"Yes, in a year. I would like that," I smiled in my sleep.

"No, not in a year- now. I'm going to convince your mom that we should enter a foreign exchange program for our senior year."

"Mmm- she'll never agree to it, especially not after this."

"Yes- she will. She'll think you need it, after what happened. I'm going to go work on her right now."

"At three in the morning?" I squinted at the clock on my heart monitor. My heart beat made a steady rhythm on the screen.

"That's the best time of day."

"You aren't going to bite her to convince her are you?"

"No. I like your mom. Sinead?"

"Hmmm," I said.

"We have a lot in common, and I don't want to lose you. I'm making a promise that I will be a safe harbor to you. People like us need to stick together in this world."

"Okay- Kelly. I'll stick by you too."

Kelly pulled the covers up to my neck. She was staring at me as if she couldn't believe I was really there and talking to her. After a few moments I closed my eyes and she slipped out the door. I guess to persuade my mom while she slept. I wasn't quite sure if Kelly was serious. But if she could make it happen, I was willing to go with her.

I wasn't sure I could trust Kelly, but I knew she would try to make me happy with this trip. And despite all my misgivings about giving her a second chance, I wanted the adventure. I was going to go with her, because I always felt alive when I was with Kelly. Besides it would help me forget Martin.

Martin- who I hoped was on his way home. I tried to picture him as I last remembered him- a giant sea monster with blue scales, wavy fins and long tendrils dripping off an enormous snout. And his deep soulful eyes- they were still there, even if he didn't know me anymore. It wouldn't be difficult for him to get to the Atlantic and swim to his home which I imagined was somewhere near the Irish Sea.

Anytime my heart hurt for him, I told myself it was not meant to be. He wasn't the one for me. There would be 'the one' and I would know it. Besides- I got my best friend back and it was better this way- no distractions.

BLOOD ACROSS THE POND

The second book in the Shed Skin Trilogy due out fall 2014.

Loving someone is easy, forgiving would be the hard part.

Kelly has a lot to make up for. Not only did she try to steal Sinead's boyfriend Martin- she almost killed him in the process of changing him into a vampire. But he didn't change- at least not into a vampire.

Taking Sinead across the pond, to Scotland, so she can find out about her banshee bloodline, is just the beginning of Kelly undoing past mistakes.

Sinead dreams of selkies and meeting her banshee clan, but what starts out as an adventure in Scotland for the two girls, ends in a dangerous confrontation halfway across the globe.

Who will shed their skin next?

Visit www.michellegartner.com for more information.